The Stars Change

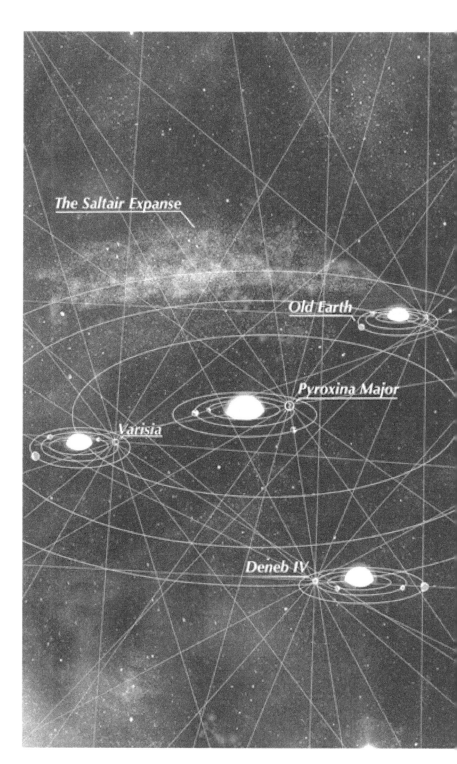

The Stars Change

by Mary Anne Mohanraj

Illustrations by Jack Kotz

Circlet Press, Inc.
Cambridge, MA

ISBN 978-1-61390-084-0 (paperback)
ISBN 978-1-61390-085-7 (ebook)

Published by Circlet Press, Inc.
39 Hurlbut Street
Cambridge, MA 02138
www.circlet.com

for *Aparna* Sharma,
who summoned *a better* future
with both hands

Sidere mens eadem mutato

The stars change
but the mind remains the same.

Contents

This is the world. This is the world he has come to destroy, a jewel of a world in the crown of the galaxy. The locals call it Kriti, which means creation. From his ship high above, he sees it all from the cabin windows. Charted Space, traced in lights against the midnight sky, worlds variously bright and dim and invisible, but there. There today, but not tomorrow. Some of those lights will die in what is to come; he has been promised that. Promised by quiet men in velvet-dressed rooms. There would be storms, there would be fire. The sturdy central core, Old Earth and its six daughters, might hold inviolate, at first. But the planets on the fringe, where alien, humod, and human mixed, where like rubbed up against unlike on a daily basis—those worlds were ripe for destruction, ready for the cleansing fire.

So said the men in the velvet rooms, grave and certain in their embroidered robes. They said Jump, and he jumped. And here he was, on a ship that had Jumped from the center to the fringe. Seven Jumps through holes across the galaxy, and now he was far, farther from home than he had ever been or wanted to be. They had paid him for his labor, had insisted. He could have wished for Old Earth coins instead of credits on his chip, thirty silver coins that he could pour from one hand to the next, that he could spill onto the floor in bitter bright profusion.

They had already paid the men, the men waiting for him, waiting for his word. The word that would send arrows arcing through the night. If only they were only arrows. The ship was landing now, circling down in a slow spiral, losing air and velocity. He fixed his eyes on the windows—he would witness this. He would witness it all, if he could do nothing else. There were the mountains, arcing around this glittering city of towering spires. Five million souls. Did aliens have souls? Did the humods? Five million souls, more or less. Less, when he was through. The city sheltered in the lee of the mountains; the peaks curved around, an upthrust hand, cradling something infinitely precious.

There were a few other cities on this world, but none nearly so large, so glittering. None so much a target. From this height, the various precincts were clearly marked. The medical complex, bright and white and vast. The mathematical eyrie clung to the side of a mountain, not far below the astronomer's peak. The psychologists had built themselves a maze to navigate; mastering it was a graduation requirement. The tower of art centered the campus, a frothy creation of violet spun-steel. And the historians lived within an immense Mughal palace, a testament to the glories of their ancestors. Despite his earlier years at the university, he didn't know much of the history of this world—only what everyone knew. That a small group of wealthy Indians had left Solvida, citing religious persecution, and had fled here for refuge. Had built themselves a university, a place where all faiths, all peoples, were welcome. He knew what everyone knew, and that was already more than he could bear. He hadn't wanted to know more.

His destination was not so visible; his fellow programmers had buried themselves underground, for the sake of their machines. But he knew where to go. To the eastern edge of campus, near the Warren, where the monsters lived. Avian, saurian, gasbags, methane breathers—all the bizarre variations the universe had offered up, once humans escaped the confines of Old Earth. All the aliens that could survive on a planet's surface, in human-comfortable temperatures, at any rate. Just west of the Warren, lay the entrance to the programmer's lair, a massive gate of metal wrought in fantastic shapes. He had the key. The men would be waiting.

Part I: These Days of Peace

Haec otia fovent studia:
These days of peace
foster learning

The Night Air

Not fucking again. Literally fucking, which was the problem—Kimmie's upstairs neighbors, the skinny brown human and the curvy gold human, were at it again. For what, the fourth time tonight? The management could claim however much it wanted that the walls were supposed to be sound-proofed; the truth was that this was a shitty apartment, it clearly wasn't up to code, and when two grown adults decided to hurl their bodies together on a battered wooden bed, you could hear it. You would think after getting the news that the war was finally on, after years of hate-mongering and human-supremacist-group posturing, the pair would have gone decently to sleep, but no. They were probably celebrating life or some such bullshit. Kimmie couldn't take it anymore. She shoved back the chair from her desk, grabbed a fur to wrap around herself, and headed out into the night.

She just wanted to walk, far and fast and until her brain stopped buzzing. Sometimes walking helped. The streets were more empty than usual—everyone who had someone was probably at home, cuddling them up, waiting for the bombs to fall or the shooting to start or the diseases to spread or just for the chips in their heads to catch viruses, melt, and drip out of their brains. And yeah, the truth was that if she had someone, Kimmie would probably do the same thing. But she didn't, and that alone was enough to make it easy to glare at the people who were glaring at her, as they always did when they saw her walking around wrapped in a fur. Fucking holier-than-thou types. How did they know that it wasn't synthetic? It could totally be synthetic.

It *wasn't*, but they had no way of knowing that, not unless they looked past the thick bright azure fur she'd wrapped around herself. Not unless they could look at Kimmie's own orange pelt, the pointed crimson ears jammed into a knitted cap, the clawed hands, the fucking *tail*, and correctly identify her as Varisian. Sure, if they did that, and if they then *happened* to be educated enough to be familiar with the adulthood rituals of her tribe, then they might recognize that the remains of the creature wrapped around her were, in fact, real. That it was her own kill, and that she had managed to face down a dumb critter with three times her mass and armed only with what she could make herself after being dumped in the Jungle. Jungle with a capital J, because it was the only real Jungle left, huge and carefully preserved in the midst of Varisia, a world that had gone completely high-tech. And yet we still value our ancient rituals, oh yes, we care about who we are as a people, and any youngling who can't survive the way our people did a thousand years ago (when they had no fucking *choice*)—well, that kid doesn't deserve to live, does she?

Kimmie had survived it, but only just, emerging with three brutal scars scraped down her back that would tell her the weather the rest of her life. Not that she needed it here. The weather on Pyroxina Major was always the same, always programmed cool, drizzly, and supposedly-temperate—and you had to wonder what sort of colonial hang-ups these people had, that after going halfway across the galaxy, these descendants of Indians decided oh, hey, let's make sure our planet always feels just like jolly old England in the rainy damp springtime. Whose brilliant idea was that?

Everyone else seemed to like it fine, but Kimmie was always fucking freezing here, and sometimes—*truth be told, every damn day*— she wondered why she'd bothered to come here at all. This was why she hadn't just opted out of the idiotic adulthood ritual, because only those who passed it (*survived it*) were deemed by the planetary higher-ups to be acceptable representatives of their species to the outside universe. So fine, she jumped through their hoops, because if there was one thing she had wanted, with the burning passion of a thousand white dwarf suns, it was to go to the University of All Worlds on Pyroxina Major, where she could learn to program like the gods themselves. And here she was, for all the good it was doing her. So she was damn well going to wear her fur, and all the judgmental vegetarian locals could just go fuck themselves.

God, she hadn't had a steak in almost ten *years*. It would be ten years after the semester and the subsequent monsoons ended. More fucking rain. Ten years of eating synthetic meat, and you could taste the difference with every bitter bite, no matter what they said. Her advisor had told her, sympathetically, that graduate school was an exercise in deprivation. And she had *tried*, goddess knows, but this place had climbed into her brain, colonized her inside and out. She didn't even think of herself by her real name anymore, Kimsriyalani, but instead as Kimmie, a name that got plastered to her by an idiot grad student who touched her fur on the first day of orientation and said loudly, smiling, that the orange shade reminded him of his mother's kim-chee, and that if she didn't mind, he'd just call her Kimmie.

And the worst of it was that he had been drop-dead gorgeous, and Kimmie had been lonely, and she had said yes, Kimmie would be fine, and she smiled up at him. She did like a tall man. And that had cost her five years of work.

She'd dated the bastard, helped him with his pathetic research, and then he'd bolted, taking her best results with him and claiming them for his own. He was clever with faking computer data, she had to give him that. Clever at manipulating people. Clever at all sorts of things that didn't involve actually working. And so, five years in, she'd started all over. New topic, new research, and a new resolve not to make the same mistake again. Kimmie'd gone on the offense, finally, switched from defense systems to weapons, and although she'd never admit it to her mother, with all her painful glorying in their supposed warrior heritage, Kimmie had to admit to herself that she had a knack for weapon systems. They were intoxicating in their beauty, their power. When she sank into the depths of the code, she felt on the verge of drowning, or flight.

A vow of celibacy had helped, along with a hell of a lot of time in the lab. Kimmie was almost there, too, almost ready to call it done, and now there was this stupid. fucking. war. She wasn't ready, and what idiots thought they could pull off an interstellar war anyway? Too big, too expensive, too likely to blow up in their faces. Not to mention, too fucking speciesist. Varisia was many Jumps away, and well-defended, at least in theory. But they'd never actually had to *use* their ships and defense grid against a horde of humans. There were just so damn many humans. The war was being pushed by a fringe group now, just three of the human-settled planets in alliance against the universe, or at least the non-human/humod parts of it. But if all the humans joined in, Kimmie knew, in the cold center of her chest, that her people were unlikely to survive.

Kimmie stopped walking, wrapped her arms even more tightly around herself. She was on a path in some park she'd never seen before, surrounded by trees, the light of the moons barely making it through the dense leaves. Dark enough that the humans would barely be able to see at all, though she had no such trouble. It would be a good place to cry, but she hadn't cried in a long time. She'd held herself together by sheer force of will, but now—now Kimmie couldn't take it anymore. She'd been running the same damn loop in her head for five years now, obsessing over what she'd done, what she'd done wrong, and what good had it done her? It had let her focus on her work, sure, wrapped up in bitterness and despair, and that might be good for science, but it kind of sucked for her. She walked up to a nearby tree and slowly, deliberately, started banging her forehead against it. Her fur cushioned the blows, but still, they hurt. Bang. Bang. Bang. It was a *good* pain, she tried to tell herself. It was better than feeling nothing at all. Bang. Bang. Bang.

"Hey—are you all right?"

He was tall; he was dark. He wasn't exactly handsome, with ears that stuck out and oddly thick glasses in a world where almost everyone got that sort of thing corrected. But he wasn't bad either, and Kimmie had stopped trusting handsome a long time ago. This one looked—nice. He'd stopped a careful distance away, far enough not to be threatening, close enough not to have to shout.

Perfect judgement, really. Maybe that was why she turned fully around, took five long strides up to within an inch of him, tilted her head up and said, "Fuck me, please."

"Miss?" he asked, clearly totally bewildered, and that was charming too, the odd archaic term coming out of nowhere. And she knew she shouldn't, but he could walk away if he wanted to—he was bigger than she was, maybe even stronger (although maybe not, you never knew with these humans, they could be surprisingly fragile)—and she just didn't care. Kimmie was up on her toes and carefully, quickly, pressing her lips against his, mouth open, breathing her breath into his mouth. Thank goddess almost nothing crossed the species barrier—one less thing to worry about, and maybe there was at least one benefit to dating humans after all. He hesitated for one breath more and then oh, thank you thank you thank you, he was kissing her back, his arms coming around her, so that she felt free to do the same, the fur falling to the ground, and moments later, she was pulling him down onto it, and he came down with her, willingly.

She peeled out of her jumpsuit as fast as she could, trusting him to manage his own clothes—human clothes always had so many weird little buttons and laces and zippers and things. And then they were naked, wrapped around each other, rolling on the ground—and no, they didn't stay on the fur, it wasn't *that* big, but it didn't matter, the grass was great too, soft and thankfully dry. When he pushed into her, he stopped, surprised, and started to ask, "You're not—" and she said "No, no, it's just been a long time. A *really* long time." That seemed to be enough explanation for him, so she didn't have to go on to explain how Varisian females were built a little more compactly inside than human females—oh, the bastard had loved that—but she wasn't going to think about him anymore. Not with this man, this *gentleman*—because she didn't know his name and she had to call him something inside her own head and if he could be archaic, so could she—not with him sliding all the way in, his mouth hot on hers, his hands digging into her furry ass.

This gentleman was not being so gentle anymore, now that he was buried in her to the hilt and oh, goddess. Oh, please. Why the fuck had she been so *stupid* for so long? It seemed as if he were somehow inside every inch of her, from head to fingers to toes, like stars exploding as he began to move, pulling out and slamming back in again. A blazing light streaked overhead, followed by a dull explosion that shook the ground. But she barely noticed either, lost to the motion of their bodies, locked together. She writhed beneath him, and had to fight once more—it had been so long—to remember not to let her claws dig into an unguarded human back. Retract, retract, that was the rule, and she could manage it, almost—oh, there was a small scrape, and on one level she *was* sorry, but on another level she was a nova, and the nova had a name, and it was Kimsriyalani! and she would never ever *ever* be fucking Kimmie again.

Thick as a Brick

Gaurav leaned back against a tree, taking in the scene. The pair was on the ground now, clothes discarded, her orange-furred and muscled limbs wrapped tightly around the brown human's body. One, two, three—and then they flipped, and Gaurav was sure that she was the one who had rolled him over, so that she was now on top, her torso upright now, arching in the dappled moonlight. Gaurav felt his pulse picking up, his breath coming thickly. Arousal a gift, after so long without, even if he could do nothing about it; the female was clearly otherwise occupied. She was a beauty, the Varisian—magnificent. One of his human colleagues wouldn't be able to see that much, not from this distance, not at night. But his eyes were far better than human, which was an advantage when your captain assigned you to the night watch for the third month in a row.

In ordinary times, Gaurav might complain of unfair treatment, might even lodge a complaint of species discrimination. Captain Raj had made enough disparaging remarks that the whole station knew that the captain had it in for the non-humans among them. *Jelly-heads have jelly for brains. You can't trust something with tentacles where arms should be.* The captain's favorite, repeated so often that even the lowest cadet could repeat it verbatim, was the all-purpose: *If they come where they're not wanted, they should expect trouble.* The captain usually avoided the saurian-specific humor when Gaurav was in the same room. Usually. *How many lizards does it take to screw in a lightbulb? None— they fall asleep first. Ha ha ha.* In ordinary times, that sort of thing could get even a senior officer fired—but not now. These days, Gaurav kept his head down and tried to do his job.

And tonight—tonight was a night for every non-human on the planet to keep his, her, or its mouth shut. No one had seen this coming; no one had thought that the Human First movement would ever progress beyond a few scattered bombs, a hate-filled rally or two. But over the last year, the movement had grown at frenetic, unbelievable pace. Serious money must be behind it, and their bought politicians had won elections in three separate planets—all in the same system, but still, a shock. And now those planets had declared war, and the rest of the Charted Worlds had no idea how serious the threat might be—so tonight, everyone was on edge. Waiting for the ball to drop.

Technically, Gaurav's job required that he haul these two in; screwing in a campus park was illegal, no matter how secluded it was. Normally, he would have done his job, arrested them, let them cool down in what passed for a cell in the campus police station. But hell. Gaurav had bigger things to worry about tonight; he didn't want to be tied up doing paperwork when he should be out here, smelling the air. His old partner had always said that a real cop smelled the air, listened to the night. Kris should know, since he'd actually been a real cop, before retiring from the city's force and joining the campus police.

Kris said campus policing wasn't that different—at least not here, where the University of All Worlds took up almost as much space as the rest of the capital city. Between the twenty-block legal and diplomatic institute, the thirty-block medical research complex, and the sprawling madness of undergrad and grad departments whose programs had colonized buildings as far as even the reptilian eye could see, the University was its own little sub-city. With its bright and shiny upper class—the aforementioned diplomats and doctors—and its dingy underbelly. The non-human sector, the Warren. Gaurav lived there too. Because while there was no regulation requiring that non-humans live in the Warren, the locals sure didn't make it easy to live anywhere else.

She really fucked beautifully, orange fur and all; it was a pleasure to watch her. Torment too. It had been a long time for Gaurav. Four months, two weeks, six days since that 'flyer bomb had gone off. The worst part, the very worst, was that it hadn't even been meant to explode—not at that particular moment. The moment when Kris was there on his 'cycle, hovering two meters away, pulling that man over for a stupid expired registration. But the man had panicked, or maybe the homemade, jury-rigged misbegotten excuse for a bomb had just failed. They'd never know; all Gaurav knew was that he'd ended up picking up the pieces of his partner and occasional bed-mate from the pavement a hundred meters below.

In the wrong place at the wrong time, but that was a cop's job, wasn't it? To go stick his pointy, scaly nose into all the wrong places, just to see what might explode. That's what Kris said. Their job to walk the front lines, so ordinary citizens could sleep safe and oblivious in their beds.

Gaurav hadn't used to think that way—he'd taken this job be-cause it was a job, that's all. Something to pay the bills. When he'd started, Gaurav figured that if he ran into any trouble, he would turn around and run the other way. He'd ended up on this world by mistake; it was just supposed to be a stopover on his ceremonial tour of the known galaxy, a reward from his parent-clutch for fin-ishing his schooling. He'd landed routinely, toured the famed Uni-versity city, and been ready and waiting for his next ship. But then the navigator on the liner he'd been scheduled to take out of Pyroxina had somehow, terribly, miscalculated on its way in; the ship had Jumped into nowhere, taking almost a thousand crew and passengers with it. Leaving Gaurav shocked and stranded here when the liner's parent corporation refused to refund his ticket. He'd signed the waiver; he'd known the risks.

It wasn't a bad place to be stranded. Cold for his liking, but the people were nice enough. *Had* been nice enough, before all this trouble started. Surprisingly traditional, many of them, and mostly vegetarian, which he really couldn't understand. His people didn't have that option, even if they'd wanted it. Kris had explained some of the history during the long nights on patrol, how the first wave of South Asian immigrants from Old Earth had been religious refugees. They'd been homesick, Gaurav supposed, had clung to the old traditions as a way of reminding themselves of who they were. Religion, clothing, language, food.

He could understand that, the homesickness. Sometimes Gaurav missed his parent-clutch's den fiercely, and the poor efforts he'd made towards reproducing the cave in his standard-issue apartment were revealed for the meager illusion they were. A few grey sheets tacked onto the walls, some red heat lamps, were no substitute for the real thing. Not without the warmth of a body beside you at least, warming your nest. Sometimes, in the darkest nights, Gaurav dragged extra sheets into his bed, molded them into the semblance of a figure, just to have something to hold on to.

Now, of course, a few hundred years after its colonization, this planet had shaken off much of that longing, that holding on. The children only half-understood their parents' yearnings, and the grandchildren had no idea at all. A hundred splinters arose from the original three religions, and non-human influence brought in completely new ones as well. But more than anything else, the discovery that this planet was a wormhole hub, linked to a dozen different worlds, and the growth of the university in response, had changed everything. The university had forced flexibility on what might otherwise have become an insular, rigid little planet.

Gaurav would have liked to go to university, but he wasn't smart enough to get in. *Thick as a brick*, Captain Raj used to say. Gaurav was built like a brick too, bigger and stronger than most humans. Big and strong were advantages for a cop. He was slower-moving than the captain would have liked. But most days, all that a campus cop needed to do was loom in a threatening manner, so Gaurav did okay. Looming. Waiting for something better to come along.

He'd just been marking time until Kris arrived, forcibly retired from the real force at eighty, but still too energetic, too passionate, to spend his days knitting at home. Energetic enough to still do extra training, and harass him into doing it too, until Gaurav could almost keep up with him. Passionate enough to drag his bewildered partner into bed on occasion, and hadn't *that* been a surprise. The first time still inscribed, sharp as a hunter's tooth, in his memories.

Gaurav had been in the patrol car at the end of a long shift, complaining: "You just don't understand how hard it is, being the only saurian on the planet." He was a whiny brat back then, two years on the job and technically an adult, but with too many habits of adolescence.

"Oh, I'm sure you're not the only one; it's a big planet." Kris answered absently, his eyes fixed on the screens, scanning the readouts for trouble.

"The only one I've seen in three years!" He sighed. "If I don't get back home, it's going to shrivel up and fall off."

That got Kris to turn to face him, finally. "Do they do that?" he'd asked.

"No, not really! It's an expression!" Didn't humans know *anything* about any species other than their own?

Kris raised a slender eyebrow. "Maybe you should go visit a professional. Some of them are quite open-minded. There's one down on Iskander Road, Chieri—"

He shook his head. He wasn't that desperate. Not yet.

A funny, slow smile slid across Kris's face. "Too proud to pay for it, huh? Well, maybe a man could help a lizard out." And that was when Kris reached out, across the 'flyer's gearshift, and put his hand on him. Right there. Gaurav almost crashed the damned machine.

Gaurav had known even then that humans would look askance at their mutual gratification. For one thing, they didn't seem to approve of large age differences between sexual partners, and Kris was almost sixty years older than he was. But Gaurav had a hard time telling how old humans were, anyway—there were enough youths coloring their hair that a white-crowned head was no reliable indicator. Kris was a little wrinkly, it was true—but nowhere near as wrinkly as Gaurav was. He could only see the difference if Kris were standing right next to a young human his own age. So age wasn't a problem for the two of them. Or gender—Gaurav's people were generally flexible. The species thing did pose a few difficulties; for one thing, Kris was surprised by how slow Gaurav was, in everything. And more than once, Gaurav had misjudged his own strength and bruised his partner. But Kris adapted beautifully. And when the captain really cut loose on Gaurav, Kris would whisper wickedly in Gaurav's cold ear that Kris *liked* him thick as a brick. Gaurav had loved Kris a little for that.

What Kris really loved were the students, hapless as they so often were. He'd cared so damn much about them, he'd made Gaurav care too. Gaurav even knew this one—Kimmie. A grad student, a programmer; she worked with security systems, which was almost as if they worked in the same field, though he knew Kimmie was a hell of a lot smarter than he was. She often worked late but never called for escort home. He and Kris had kept an eye on her anyway, as they could, had exchanged friendly chat when they passed in the night. She was graduating this year, on her way out. He'd never thought to see the girl like this, naked on the ground. Beautiful, though. Good for her—Kris would have approved of her passion.

Kris probably wouldn't approve of Gaurav playing voyeur, though. *If it isn't your business, go find something that is.* That was one of the things he used to say a lot. Gaurav's mouth quirked into a sad smile at the thought, and then he turned away from the pair flailing on the ground. Even though Kris was four months gone, his mark was on him, indelible. Gaurav thought he might spend the rest of his life trying not to let Kris down.

In that moment of turning, a light flashed across the sky. Followed by a horrible, hollow boom from the heart of the Warren. From his home—the buildings composed of thin wood walls, so fragile, compared to the rock of a proper den. A moment later, fire blazed up, a pillar in the air. Gaurav's heart jumped into his throat. With all the speed he could muster, he ran straight toward the blaze.

Crackles and Chokes

The woman had smelled like dust, like dry, hot nights and parched dirt. That was what Rajiv remembered most, along with the fur—how could he not remember the fur? It was like making love under a blanket, but outside, skin bare to the cool, damp air. She—he hadn't learned her name—moved beneath him hot and fierce, sharp as a crackle of ozone in the air, a lightning bolt slicing down, piercing through his center. And then, just as they'd finished and she had rolled away, the missile streaked through the sky above them, landing, gods, too close. He could imagine the rubble, the devastation. The screams.

For long minutes, Rajiv had waited, frozen naked on the ground, waited to see if there would be more, if this was the opening salvo in a rain of destruction that would kill them all. But there had been no more. Just the one. Several miles away, it looked like, too far away to even feel the impact—but on the university grounds, almost certainly, and the shock of that coursed through him. The woman disappeared, without a word, leaving him alone. Rajiv went home. When he walked in the door, took off his clothes and climbed into bed beside his sleeping wife, he could still feel electricity pulsing under skin that seemed too small, too tight, to contain his body. He had to discharge that energy. He rolled his wife over—gently—and began to make love to her.

He loved to wake Amara up like this. Heavy with sleep, her thick body a weight in their bed like a marble statue, and he Pygmalion, bringing her to life. Sometimes he would start with lips against the back of her neck, a hand wound in her mass of black hair, tugging her head back, to give his mouth better access. She always said at night that she should braid it for sleeping, but she was too tired, too sluggish from her long day at the port, processing visas for what seemed an unending stream of visitors—

students, parents, tourists, traders, business folk. All of that would stop now, Rajiv suddenly realized. There would be nothing for her to do, until the war ended.

He hoped Amara didn't start braiding her hair. Rajiv liked it like this, dense and loose, and when she woke up in the morning, cursing at the tangles, he liked to help her brush them out. She would sit, cross-legged on the carpet at the foot of the bed, and he would sit on the bed behind her, tugging gently at the mess he had helped create. Now he lay beside her on the bed, twisted the fingers of one hand in her hair, but didn't pull—not yet. Rajiv didn't want to wake her that way. He started with a kiss instead, a kiss for his princess, his sleeping beauty. Amara had no patience for the stories in his head; she said that wasn't why she'd married him, to listen to his endless stories. He said, if she didn't like stories, why had she married an English professor? And she just shook her head, impatiently.

Her mother had arranged the match, of course—she'd cared less about his interest in books and more in the size of his salary. But it wasn't as if Amara hadn't agreed to it. Probably she was just as involved in sorting through the possibilities as her mother was, but he would never know for sure. She would never admit it. Amara was a traditional sort of girl, the kind of girl he'd thought he'd wanted. Beautiful, skilled in the domestic arts, fond of children; a good sort of wife for an ambitious young professor. They'd wanted, expected, children, and maybe if they'd had them, she would have stayed happy in the life she chose. But they hadn't been blessed, and eventually, they stopped trying. Her family didn't believe in genetic interventions; they followed one of the more traditional branches of Hinduism, and tried to accept what the gods fated for them. Rajiv had never been able to resign himself so calmly.

Rajiv's lips pressed against his wife's, gently urging them apart. He breathed her air, thick with sleep and still faintly laced with the cloves she chewed before bed. She still chewed cloves instead of using a sonic toothbrush. Backward, barbaric practices—he didn't know why Amara insisted on living as if she were still back on Earth, five hundred years ago. Living like her great-great-many-times-great-grandmother had. She talked of religion, of tradition, of fate. All Rajiv knew was that it would take no more than an hour in a doctor's office to fix all their problems—she could walk in, have a simple procedure, and be growing a child. Their child. It would be so easy. His fist clenched in her hair.

Amara's eyes opened beneath him, startled. Her mouth opened, as if to speak, but he didn't give her the chance. He thrust his tongue in instead, plunging deep into the heat of her barbaric mouth. Rajiv rolled his body on top of hers, pushing up her thin cotton nightgown with fevered hands, urging her legs apart. And Amara opened for him, her legs moving apart, her arms coming up to encircle him. His mouth still hard on hers, he thrust himself into her, only in that moment remembering the other woman, a bare hour before. For a moment, he wasn't sure whom he was with, which woman he was fucking. And then he was back, back with his wife, one hand lost in her hair, and the other digging into her ass, pulling her to him with each mindless thrust.

Afterwards, she pulled away. Amara sat up in bed, pulling her nightgown down, the sheets up, a barricade. "Why do you taste like that?" she asked him. Her voice was thin and tight, and her eyes were bright with sudden tears.

"Like what?" Rajiv asked.

She shook her head, her thick, tangled hair falling heavy around her shoulders. "Like—sand. Sand and dust and lightning."

Rajiv hadn't planned to tell her, but in that moment, with that missile arcing across the sky, with the memory of the two women so close together in his mind, the feel of them, skin and fur, sparks and tears, blurring together, he couldn't say anything but the truth.

He said, "I had sex with someone else. A woman I met in the park. I don't know her name." And then Rajiv watched his wife get out of bed, pull on sandals and a jacket, and pull a bag out of the closet. Already packed—it took her no more than three minutes. How long had Amara had a bag packed, ready to carry with her out the door? They didn't have the best marriage—Rajiv knew that. His wife wasn't exactly happy. But he'd never expected her to leave him.

It was only when Amara put her hand to the front door lock, letting it read her print and silently slide open, that he opened his mouth to ask, incredulous, "You're leaving?" How could his so-traditional wife walk out? Their marriage was written in fire and stone; she was supposed to think of him as her own personal incarnation of god. That was what she'd always said she believed, even when he'd mocked the very idea. Could a follower just abandon her god?

"What did you think would happen?" Amara asked wearily, before walking out, letting the door slide silently shut behind her.

Past Echoes

Amara ran. She had started out walking, her steps slow but steady. Walking away from the exploded ship that had been her marriage. It hadn't been spaceworthy in a long time, leaking air, on the verge of decompression. But she had held on, slapping patches up as fast as she could, holding the ship together with wire and prayers and dogged determination—no one could ever accuse her of lacking willpower. She had committed to this marriage, and she had been determined to see it through. Until Rajiv had come home stinking of another woman, and blown a hole right through the heart of it.

She'd known about his earlier affairs, of course. He was a terrible liar. Amara had known, but she hadn't been able to tell anyone, hadn't even been able to really face them herself. It was too humiliating. Especially since *she* had been the one to insist on a traditional, old-Earth marriage, complete with vows of lifetime loyalty. Rajiv would have been fine with a standard five-year renewable contract—if she'd signed that, then she would have been free to walk away at the end of the term, honor intact. But instead, Amara had forced him to marry her for life. And then she was stuck with the results.

It was all Narita's fault. It was ironic to think this, as Amara's sandals slapped the wet pavement that led her, inexorable as a ship in the middle of Jump, down the three miles of deserted university walkways to Narita's shabby door. Ironic, but the truth. If Narita hadn't done what she did, then Amara would never have gone to her so-traditional mother and asked her to arrange her marriage.

It had happened on a night just like this one—wet and windy. The semester had just ended and the monsoon rains had started; WeatherAdmin always waited until the students were gone before turning up the rain. There was no real need for monsoons on this planet, of course, but people were nostalgic for the old days. When you came as an immigrant, a stranger in a very strange land, you did everything you could to hold on to home. Even when home changed beyond all recognition, immigrants held on to the vision of what it had once been, and passed that vision on to their descendants.

That was what Rajiv said, anyway, usually when he was trying to talk Amara in doing things his way, instead of the way her family had always done things. Her family wasn't rich, but it was old— her great-great-grandfather had been one of the first settlers. Her mother still wore chappals outside and bare feet in the house; she dressed in sari daily. Intricate jali-work and inlaid brass graced their furniture. Her family patronized the small local artisans who still hand-crafted clothes and furniture the old way; it would be cheaper to buy modern, mass-produced goods, but her mother always said such things lacked soul. And yes, traditions had some-times adapted to their new planet—her parents were life-long veg-etarians, but in the old days, her father had been known to enjoy an imitation vat-steak with his friends from the shipyard. You adapted, or you died. But you held on to as much of the past, of your history, as you could.

Her family had always been proud of their traditions, and Amara was still proud of them—most of them, anyway. All of them except for the one that had ruined her life. Her bag slapped against her damp thigh and she pulled it up into her arms, holding it close, like a child, as she ran. Not much in the old grey bag—just a change of clothes and a few legal documents. Her marriage license. Her credit pass. Just what she needed to start her life over again, to cor-rect the moment when she'd taken the wrong fork in the road.

That night, the wind had risen, but neither Amara nor Narita had minded. They were in Narita's tiny apartment, as usual— Amara still lived with her mother, since she couldn't afford to move out. Not unless she wanted to take a manual labor job in one of the terraforming sectors. No, thank you. She'd managed to pull just-barely-passing grades at University, enough to get her degree, and that had qualified her for an entry-level job at the port.

She'd been there for a year now, long enough to be thoroughly bored by the work. Still, it was a job, and after work, there was Narita to see. Two years of sneaking around, successfully hiding the entire relationship. Her mother thought she was spending her evenings studying at the library; she'd been so proud that Amara had graduated university, the first in their family to manage it. Her mother still had hopes that she might manage a higher degree. Amara didn't have the heart to disillusion her, especially when the library provided such a convenient excuse.

That night, they'd been wet inside and out. While the wind and rain whipped against the apartment's single window, they slid together, naked and slippery as Illurian eels. Twining together in a practiced dance, their bodies oddly similar in build. Thin, small-breasted, with narrow, oval faces, long, muscled legs and waist-length hair that both women usually wore in the single traditional braid down the back. People sometimes mistook them for sisters. But no one who saw them now could make that mistake, not with Narita's mouth hot on Amara's breast, Narita's two, three, four fingers pushed up, inside the pulsing wet center of Amara's world.

It was blazingly hot in the apartment—the temperature controls were out again—and they were drenched with sweat. Maybe that was why they finally managed it that night, after months upon months of trying—four fingers slid out and five slipped in, Narita's mouth whispering eager encouragement into Amara's ear. *Come on, relax, you can do it, open for me, come on, come on!* Pushing and twisting, slick and insistent, that one stubborn knuckle resisting until pop! she was in. Like magic. And once Narita was inside, that hand opened like a flower, like the fabled jethamine that bloomed only once every hundred years. Was there really such a thing? Amara didn't know—she only knew that she was lost, unmoored, cast adrift on a waves of pleasure that came again, and again, and again. That refused to end until at last, exhausted, she begged for mercy. *Please, please, no more.*

Laughing, Narita relented, sliding out and shaking her hand. *Aches*, she'd admitted. *You earned that ache*, Amara said, laughing too, now that she had a chance to catch her breath. And that was when the smile had slipped away on Narita's face, when her eyes had suddenly caught and held Amara's, when she had whispered, *Partner me*. And worse—*Have a child with me*.

After two shared years of intimacy, of intensity, how had she not guessed that Narita might eventually want that? But she hadn't, or she hadn't wanted to admit it to herself. Amara felt the air sucked out of her, her remaining breath and pulsing blood suddenly too close to the fragile barrier of skin. She'd practically jumped off the bed, had pulled her shift on with a quick motion, wrapped the half-sari and pinned it closed, slid on her sandals and was out the door, leaving Narita naked behind her, her hand still sticky-wet, her face stricken.

Amara couldn't ignore the similarity to her recent departure from her house, her marriage. But it wasn't the same. Leaving Narita had been an act of desperate panic—a mistake. Leaving Rajiv had been a relief, a longed-for release from nine long years, from the words of a contract that had begun to strangle her. Oh, she had crafted that trap for herself, had asked for a life-marriage so that she wouldn't be tempted to go back, knowing that her parents would never understand, never forgive if she chose Narita. Narita who might look human on the surface, might even look like she could be Amara's sister. But whose genes had been engineered to be stronger, smarter, faster—even prettier than normal. Modified human; humod. Sacrilege and blasphemy carved into her blood and bones.

Amara had panicked; she had run. But now, finally, she was free to run back to where she should have always been. Free to stand, shaking, on Narita's doorstep, with the strange, unseasonable wind whipping around her, the heavy rain driving icy needles against her back. Something was wrong with the weather—but it didn't matter now. Amara raised a hand, laid one cold finger on the doorplate. She barely had time to catch a breath before the door slid open just a few centimeters, showing just a fragment of that lovely face, untouched by the decade between.

"I'm sorry—you can't come in." The face was the same, but the voice sounded different. Older. The voice wasn't angry, but it was final.

"Wait—" Amara shouted the word. But it was too late; the door slid closed, and she was left standing there, clutching her old grey bag, with absolutely no idea what to do next.

Hammer in the Dark

The human female, Narita, turned back to Jequith after the door slid shut. "I'm so sorry."

"You did not have to turn away your friend, just because we are here." Jequith said the words politeness demanded, but it was intensely grateful that there were no more humans crowding into this small space. One was more than enough. The scent of this one alone, heightened by adrenaline and endorphins, was so thick that Jequith could barely think. Its mother had been right—it had been a fool to leave their world, to come to such a strange, human-filled place. Over ninety-nine percent of this planet was human populated, and yet that wasn't enough for them. They had to have it all.

Narita frowned. "Amara…wouldn't have understood. Her family are traditionalists—they're the same as the people who sent a missile into the Warren, who blew up your home. Terrorists!"

Jequith frowned. Even in the midst of its anger, its rage, with the smell of burning wood and flesh still etched in its memory, Jequith could not help but be fair. Its academic training kicked in, even now. "Not the same, surely. Not every traditionalist is anti-alien—and even among those humans who dislike and fear non-humans, most won't turn to violence. Not unless they are pushed." It was puzzling—bewildering, really. Jequith wondered, even now, in the midst of chaos, just who had been pushing these people. Humans and the other species had always had their differences, but things had blown up so fast. One day, humans were shoving Varisians and Denebians in the marketplace, dropping an insult here and there; the next day, missiles streaked through the sky. "Most people want only peace." This place had been a haven of peace, not so long ago.

Narita shrugged. "Fair enough, but I still don't think we need her in here. Not tonight. Whatever's going on with Amara, she'll just have to handle it herself." Her eyes flicked back to the corner, where Jequith's partners slept their unnatural sleep. "Are you *sure* there's nothing else we can do for Shariq?"

Concern obvious on her face. Here was the evidence that not all humans were bad; Narita had taken them in, at great risk to herself.

And what did she know of Jequith, really? A friendly office floormate, someone to greet pleasantly on the way to or from department meetings. They weren't even in the same department—recent funding cuts had squeezed nonhuman medicine into the same wing as human medicine. But they were both medical professionals, and they shared a similar love of the alien, the other. She specialized in avian diseases, and Jequith was completely fascinated by human sexuality and procreation. So Jequith had come here, to study and treat them, and now it paid the price.

It tried to reassure her. "Trust me. What there is for such as us to do, we have done." They had bound its mate's wound, made a nest where she could huddle with Harim, their male partner. "If Shariq is to heal, our mate will have to do the rest." The human still frowned, and Jequith took a quick breath and made an effort to sound more reassuring. "I am reasonably certain that she will be fine." It was telling the truth. The wound was serious, but not life-threatening, not now that they had help, and a quiet place for male and female to share the healing trance.

"And the baby?" Narita asked, frowning.

Well. That was the question.

Three years ago, Shariq had come to it. Jequith had long ago given up hope. It had known that taking this position was risky, that few of its people would be likely to come so far. Eiskiyarien, its home planet, lay seven Jumps away—for a traditional people, not given to overmuch risk, that was seven Jumps too many for most of them. Jequith had always known that it was strange, with its fascination for the foreign, the peculiar. Its parents had been united, the three of them, in warning Jequith away from this life-path. But

Jequith had been stubborn. And then, after sixteen lonely years on this planet, it had become convinced that it would pay the price for its stubbornness. To die alone, unmated, childless. It loved its work, but it had always wanted a family too. It had just hoped, expected, to be lucky, for no good reason.

And then Shariq had sashayed into its office one day, frills flared, skin flushed a dark, rich purple. She'd trilled a wordless invitation, and Jequith had been utterly bewildered. It could not give the female what she so clearly needed. Who was she? What was she *doing* here? And then Harim had sidled in behind her, shyly. He was the one who spoke. "We've been looking for you," he said. "We need you."

It was not the human way, Jequith knew, to mate so suddenly. But sometimes, there was no need for courtship, no need even for speech. They were alone, the three of them, far from their people. She was in need, and they were both willing, eager. In Jequith's sharp urgency, it barely remembered to shut the door. The threesome could have been disastrous, but as Shariq sang her mating song and they sank to the floor of Jequith's cold, barren office—so different from a mating nest back home!—it felt oddly convinced that they would, in fact, be perfect together. Finally, after all its long wanderings, Jequith had found a home.

Bang! Bang! Bang! Jequith was jerked back to the present by a renewed pounding on the door. Across the room, Shariq shivered and Harim wrapped himself more tightly around her—Jequith could scent the changes in its mates, the birthing hormones still so high in its system that it felt almost as if it were inside their skins. This was what it was for, to defend against all dangers while male and female was immersed in their new creation. Three years it had watched over them, as Shariq—so slowly!—grew the new one within her.

Three years of rising tension, as the pro-human sentiment rose, and so often it had wanted to take them away—but where could they go? Shariq could not endure a Jump with the little one within her, and there would be no point to taking a slow shuttle to one of the other planets in system, barren rocks that they were. So they were trapped on this planet until the child was born, trapped in its only major city, the single place where they could live and work in relative peace. Jequith, who had chosen to train as a scholar-medic, leaving it with no fighting skills at all, was left to twist in the wind, what little there was of it in this climate-controlled environment. Once, this planet had seemed a paradise to it, a haven for peaceful learning amidst some of the strangest peoples in the universe. A paradise—but now, it had become their prison.

And again, *Bang!* Jequith felt its vestigial outer teeth filling with poison; its body reacted, regardless of its will. Though what was the point? Now, when the child was lost to them. It could fight the woman outside the door, but even if she hated it and its people, what would be the point of fighting? There were too many humans on this planet. Even if its body were demanding that it rip the woman into bloody pieces, that it defend its mates against all comers, it would never be able to take all the humans down. There had to be another way through this war.

Bang! Jequith dug a clawed hand into its trembling thigh and snapped, "She cannot heal with these distractions; we must have quiet!" *Bang!* And then Shariq's body rippled, and Jequith felt a frantic pulse rip through its own body, in mirror to hers, a wave of motion and heat from claws to spine to armored nose. The child, still moving after all!

The little one had been still for so long after the explosion that ripped open a wall of their sleeping alcove and threw Shariq across the room with the force of the blast, hard, into the far wall. A wall-lamp pierced her side, sending blood streaming out to stain the wood floor. Harim plastered himself against her at once, so that his body might work to heal hers, merging in the way that only males and females could. And somehow, somehow Jequith managed to get them on a makeshift travois, cursing the weakness of its fore-limbs all the while. Averting its eyes from the ruin of the beautiful house they'd built together, an island of light and color in the dark streets of the Warren. Trying to ignore the breaking of its heart.

Jequith had dragged them out of the district, through the harried, frantic crowds, had brought them here, to Narita's home. Suddenly, another sweet shiver raced through it, echoing Shariq's. Jequith had assumed the child was dead, but now its throat clutched with unbearable hope. *Bang!*

"Open the door," Jequith said, its voice shaking.

Narita shook her head, protested, "Why? Why would you risk it?"

Jequith had no answer for her—there was no reason to trust, not really. But it had been granted shelter tonight, and then joy, when all hope had fled. How could it leave someone out in the cold on a night like this? "Just open it. Let her speak, at least."

Narita stood still for a long moment, as if she fought her own inner battle. And then, sighing, something loosened inside her. Her scent changed, a trickle of something sweet joining the dark scents of fear and grief. She laid her palm against the plate and the door hissed open; and the human female fell inside, one fist still raised to hammer against the door. Narita snapped, "Amara—what are you *doing* here?"

The woman had fallen against the door, but there was no lack of pride in her; she struggled back upright before answering, a bag clutched tightly to her chest. "I left him."

"What's that to me?" Narita asked. Her voice as cold as the ice that covered half of Eiskiyarien now, and her body barred the entrance, so that the woman, Amara, stood half in and half out, preventing the door from sliding shut.

"Please, kunju. Don't." It was in her voice, the desperation that her squared off shoulders denied. Amara took a quick, steadying breath. Then she said, her voice now controlled and carefully blank, despite the bleakness of her words—"I have nowhere else to go."

Jequith grieved for her, for the pain it heard. It grieved for all of them. Before Narita could answer, Jequith spoke, its hearts thumping in steady unison. "It is your home. But for our part, we would have her stay." If they were to forge a new path forward, perhaps this was part of the answer. That small creatures, desperate and despairing, should reach out to each other in the darkness of night.

Amara's eyes widened, as she finally looked beyond her own troubles to the rest of the room. Shariq and Harim in the corner, dark blood staining their clothes. Jequith, frill raised sharp as a warrior's, and in one clawed hand, a kitchen knife. What good the knife would do it, Jequith hadn't known, but after the blast knocked it to the ground, after it struggled to its feet, it found the knife in its hand. Instinct had triumphed over civilization, and it would be so tempting, to trust instinct more.

But Jequith was determined that instinct would not rule it. It would guard, it would protect; that much, instinct would make sure of. But with the life of the child singing through it, with the birthing imminent and Shariq and Harim out of immediate danger, Jequith thought that it could afford to take a risk, could dare to be kind. To repay the chance that Narita had bought for them.

Narita hesitated a long moment, and then, finally, took a step backwards. "Come in, then. You're letting in all the cold."

And it was strangely true—Jequith could feel a blast of cold air whipping past. How odd—it was if they are home again on Eiskiyarien. Maybe the chill wind had come to greet the new one that even now was readying herself to be born. "Welcome," Jequith whispered to the coming child. The human woman took a tentative step into the room, letting the door whoosh shut behind her. If she had thought that it was speaking to her, no harm done. On this night, they could all use shelter from the storm.

she wasn't what they'd promised him, the others. they'd said she'd be beautiful beyond belief beautiful as an angel a demon a dream. and she was but she was also real. real skin hot and wet and slick against him, real sighs and gasps beneath him. and maybe she was faking those, she probably was because that's what girls like this did but that didn't matter. that part he'd expected. he just hadn't expected her to seem so real.

when he'd signed up for this, he'd been told that they weren't real. weren't really people. when he'd come to the city, when he'd seen the monsters walking the streets, he'd been reassured. they were something else. they didn't belong here, taking the place of real people. not that he could have ever gone to university, he knew he wasn't smart enough, he'd never dreamed of that. but little cassie, she was smart as a genemod monkey, everyone said. it wasn't just her big brother saying that. she should have got to go.

when that letter came, printed on real paper, she'd been so excited, so sure she'd gotten in. and then no. not a chance, not even wait-listed, not even close. it was cruel of them to print the lists, to show you just how far you'd been from having a shot at a way out. oh cassie. and they said it had nothing to do with skin color, they said everyone got a fair shot, but it couldn't be a coincidence, could it, that just 'bout every man or woman he saw in the university town was brown. pale brown, medium brown, dark brown, but brown. cassie, she was pale as moonlight, orange-red hair and bright blue eyes. blue as momma's had been.

after cassie'd taken the river road out, he'd been willing to listen to the boys with their speeches. willing to take their money and come to the city, three train lines and half a world away. it wasn't right, this place, towers spiraling overhead midst bridges thin as cobweb. airships swooping so fast through the spaces above that a man got dizzy watching them. wouldn't it be fine to ride up there! never a chance for him, but they'd sent something up, they damn well had. a sword across the sky, a shout of rage. for cassie green with river weeds tangled in her orange hair. and her so young and bright.

afterwards they'd said he deserved a reward, they'd sent him off with credits piled high on new cards, said he didn't need to come back. they'd warned him. the girls here weren't real girls but that was all they could afford; if you wanted a real girl, unmodified, you had to pay through the nose. everything was backwards in university town.

so he'd come prepared, but here he was and she was and she was everything a girl ought to be, only more so. it wasn't fair that she was everything she was, prettier than cassie and probably smarter too, even if she did earn her money flat on her back. no shame in that, honest work for honest pay and he was happy to pay her, she'd more than earned it. she smiled then and it was like the sun come up over the mountains, golden. maybe that was why he told her what he'd done, that smile that sun those mountains he was missing with all his beating heart.

that was where he ought to be. not here. not surrounded by monsters so pretty you couldn't tell where real girl ended and monster began. time to go home.

Part II: Be Human

Modalu monavanagu:

Above all, be human

Old Friends Meet

With Amara there, Narita hadn't been able to stay in the apartment for five minutes more than she had to. She hurried across the darkened square on her grocery errand, avoiding the strangers who walked the dark streets as well. It had been quiet near her apartment, but the streets were growing increasingly crowded as she headed in, towards the central quadrangle and its all-night market. All the other stores were closed, shutters closed over the glass windows, like barricades against the dark. No one seemed to want to meet eyes tonight, to smile a greeting. Not tonight. The main blaze above the Warren was out now—the police and firefighters had done their work. So far, no one had died. But the net told her that smaller fires sputtered through the city, and faint traces of smoke wisped through the air. The authorities were telling everyone to stay home, stay safe. But what if home wasn't safe anymore?

Her arms were wrapped tight around herself against the unseasonable wind and slanting rain, her mind elsewhere. Narita was remembering the argument she'd had with her mother at thirteen, walking home together after the last in a series of summer tennis lessons in the blinding sunshine. Sweat poured down her face, trickled down her back and under her bra strap; she had to fight the urge to haul up her shirt and scratch her skin raw.

She'd asked, or rather, demanded, "Why didn't you give me a better internal thermostat? You modified other things, why not that?" What she actually wanted, deep down, were huge butterfly wings growing out of her back, but even at thirteen, Narita had realized how impractical those would have been.

Her mother, Uma, smiled, brushing damp hair back from Narita's forehead with a cool hand. "Hush, child. We made sure you wouldn't get cancer or smallpox or Jovian flu. That your eyesight and hearing would be perfect. That is not the same thing as tweaking your genes, willy-nilly. When you have your own children, you'll understand—you should only make important changes to the genes. Too much changing is dangerous."

The snarky pre-teen replied, "You made me pretty, too. Was *that* important?"

Uma just shook her head, refusing to engage. "Go take a nice, cool swim. You'll feel better."

That was the end of that conversation, like so many others they'd had. Narita's mother hadn't wanted to admit that they had selected for beauty as well as health—the same choices that most humods made. Her parents would have added brains too, but they hadn't wanted to risk the madness that so often came with significantly increased intelligence. They'd picked an acceptable level of beauty, within the range of human norm—slender build, flawless skin, glossy hair. Appearing too visibly modified was gauche. Vulgar. *Did you see Savitri's daughter? Shining ruby eyes, the poor thing. That's going to be hard to accessorize.*

Sometimes, growing up, Narita would stand in front of a mirror and stare at her naked body, spread fingers against the flesh and bone, trying to figure out which parts were hers by right, and which were deliberate gifts from her parents. They'd always refused to let her see the scans. Even though, legally, she could demand access, Narita was too obedient a daughter to go so far against their wishes.

Narita had eventually been grateful that her parents hadn't chosen anything too strange for her, but in this particular moment, she could wish they had been a little less conservative in their modifications. It was freezing, and her jacket was small protection. A thick skin like Jequith's would be welcome on a night like tonight.

It had offered to go to market for her, to get enough food to fuel the sudden expansion in her apartment, but she hadn't had the heart to make it leave its injured mates and new daughter. But *someone* had to get them something to eat. When Narita had started this night, she hadn't expected an influx of houseguests—she'd planned to spend the evening reading medical journals. She was due to take her final series of exams in just a few weeks, and after that, she could call herself Dr. Narita if she chose. Dr. Narita Kandaswamy—it sounded good. Her parents would be thrilled. Even if they didn't approve of some of her other decisions.

They had never liked Amara. Or rather, they liked her fine when she was just Narita's friend, but girlfriend was unacceptable. Her mother didn't believe in crossing class lines. *Dating a woman like that will only lead to trouble. She will never be comfortable with us, no matter what you do. Don't you want a partner who can mix well with our family? If you put a lump of dirt in the stew, it will ruin the whole dish.* No one had ever accused Uma of being subtle. And as the pandit's wife, leader of the entire temple ministry for more than thirty years now, Uma was used to running things, to having her own way in everything.

Something crashed up ahead, a sharp sound, like shattering plastic, snapping her out of her distant memories. Narita paused at the intersection of University and Main, startled to see a crowd gathered around a broken shop window up ahead. They couldn't be—but yes. She took an involuntary step backwards into the shadows, bewildered. It was hard to see in the dim streetlights, but the people were clearly dragging items out of the store. Holoplayers, it looked like; Narita couldn't remember the name of the store, but it was one that specialized in electronic entertainment. Was that really what people wanted tonight? To drown out thoughts of the war with the latest holodrama? They should be home with their loved ones instead. If the world was going to end, who would choose to spend their last moments in the arms of a manufactured dream?

Narita turned away, cutting down through a side street. Better not to go anywhere near them. She still couldn't believe there were actual looters on campus; a shiver slid down her spine. Oh, there was the occasional stolen scooter, its security codes hacked, but for the most part, the university grounds were a haven of peace.

Narita had walked these streets fearlessly at night even as an undergrad, and now she knew them well enough to be able to trace
a dozen different paths from her apartment to the market. She had
lived in the same apartment for more than a decade. Since even
before she had first met Amara.

The theatre lights were dim the night they met. Narita had
gone to see the play on a whim, and was, unusually for her, alone.
It was yet another retelling of *The Ramayana*, this one in a hyper-
masculinist mode, and most of her friends would have scorned
the entire concept. But she was interested in the question of what
it meant to be male these days, when so many in her circles were
choosing mixed-gender or ab-gender forms, despite the hazards
of making major genetic changes as an adult. Perhaps Narita found
males particularly interesting because she so rarely found men
attractive.

Unfortunately, the play ended up not providing any useful in-
sights on the concepts; in fact, the entire production was pretty
horrid. So when the strange woman seated beside her muttered
dreck! at Lord Ram's entirely-too-long speech on wifely duty and
the importance of apparent fidelity, Narita was all too ready to
take joy in a kindred soul. She hissed a heartfelt *agreed!* and they
were off.

Narita kept her eyes mostly on the stage, but the two of them
kept up an irritated commentary through the rest of the play. She
was grateful that the university theatre was new and fancy enough
that each seat came with customizable sound controls—they
bought and merged privacy shields, becoming inaudible and invisible to the rest of the theatre. By the end of the production, they
were laughing out loud, and were clearly destined to be the best
of friends. Which was why it was such a shock when the house
lights came up, and Narita could finally see Amara's face clearly.
Unmodified.

She had unmodified friends, of course. Narita wasn't preju-
diced. It was just that you tended to run in the same circles, didn't
you? With the people who'd gone to the same sorts of schools,

played the same games, done the same sports (and it wouldn't be fair to compete with the unmodified anyway, would it? It would be ungracious. Tacky). So even at university, the great mixer and equalizer, when aliens made up a quarter of the classes, Narita's intimate friends and lovers had continued much as they had been throughout her life. It wasn't a deliberate choice on her part, to stick to her own kind, although she had to admit, it was also more comfortable that way. No awkwardness about splitting the bill, or going clothes shopping, or choosing a spot for spring break.

But here she was, this woman, Amara. Too short, too dark, a bright red pimple forming on the bridge of her nose. It looked like it hurt; Narita wasn't sure if they did, though. She resolved to research pimples later, when she had a chance. Because if they were going to be friends, she and this unmodified girl, she wanted to understand what Amara had to contend with. Her life was surely hard enough—she didn't need Narita making things worse with tactless comments or unthinking actions. So she resolved, and then she smiled, hoping the smile had not come too long after the lights. Apparently not, because Amara smiled back. Narita stood then, deactivating the privacy screens, and said, for the whole theatre to hear—"I'm starving! Do you want to continue this conversation over dinner?"

Amara hesitated an endless moment, and Narita wondered, almost panicked, whether some trace of discomfort had shown on her own face. That *pimple*. It was so large, so very red. But then Amara said, "That'd be great. I know this great vegan place not far away…"

Vegan. Terrific. Narita swallowed a sigh and gestured for Amara to precede her out of the row. Ladies first, please. And that was the beginning.

Narita finally made it through the twisted side streets, her head down against the stiffening wind. She hadn't seen any more looters, thankfully, and the market was open, and surprisingly intact. No one was staffing it, though they usually had a few courtesy attendants on duty to make the high-end patrons feel properly taken care of. It was fully automated tonight, and Narita thought better of the university for that—they had let the employees go home early. The fragelian berries and esterhaven mushrooms would have to take care of themselves.

It was easy enough to choose food that Jequith and its family would enjoy; she filled a basket with appropriate greens, grateful for the medical training that ensured she wouldn't accidentally poison them. Amara was harder. One part of Narita wanted to buy the most expensive treats in the store, knowing that Amara wouldn't even walk into a place like this, much less buy anything here. Wanting, perhaps, to show off a little. To show Amara what she'd walked away from, when Amara had walked away from her.

They had nothing in common, her friends had pointed out. It was true. Narita was pre-med; even though she had no need to work, she had wanted to do something useful with her life. And aliens fascinated her—the strangeness of them, the danger. Even at twenty, she'd planned to become a xeno-doc, specializing in non-human diseases. Her mother didn't quite approve—diseases were so dirty, after all. But on the other hand, *doctor* was still a title of respect. Even if you never got sick, it was nice to know there was something there to take care of you if you did. At twenty, Narita was looking forward to a prosperous and prestigious career.

Amara, on the other hand, was majoring in comparative religious studies. Sadly, it was already clear that she didn't have the intellectual chops to make it into graduate school—Amara was smart, but she didn't seem to have the discipline to focus the way an academic needed to. She was barely passing half her classes. Given that, Narita was bewildered that Amara hadn't chosen a more practical degree, something that could actually help her get a decent job after university. But Amara just said, *This is the only time in my life when I can afford not to be practical.* So she kept reading her strange texts, searching for God in increasingly bizarre places.

They couldn't study together; they couldn't shop together; they couldn't even eat together. Not comfortably. Amara's idea of a treat was to have a little spinach paneer with her everyday rice and dal, all of which she cooked herself on a little burner in her dorm room. Narita had her own apartment, with a full kitchen, paid for by her parents—but she was used to having all her meals out, in restaurants that specialized in exotic cuts of vat-meat, drenched in heavy cream sauces, and followed by sinfully rich desserts. It wasn't as if she needed to worry about her figure; that took care of itself.

The only place they had anything in common was, they discovered, in bed. Where the two of them could talk and laugh and fuck and argue for hours upon hours on end. Oddly enough, that had turned out to be more than enough for them both. Until it wasn't, and Amara walked away. Disappeared for nine years, not a call or a message, as if she'd been wiped off the face of the planet; apparently Narita was good enough to fuck, but not good enough to partner with. And now Amara was back, though Narita still didn't know why. She wasn't sure she wanted to.

Narita hesitated a long moment in front of the stasis container of imported delicacies. Plants grown under strange suns, light-years away. But in the end, good breeding reasserted itself. However angry she was, Amara was a guest in her home. A guest in trouble, on a terrible night. Narita bought rice and lentils, spinach and paneer. She didn't know how to cook them, but Amara would. Narita should head home now, let Amara get started cooking. But her stomach twisted at the very thought.

It had been Amara's turn to provide dinner, that night ten years ago. Amara cooked on her nights; Narita ordered in. That was easiest for both of them. But on that night, Amara couldn't cook— she was too sick, with the most miserable cold Narita had ever witnessed. Her nose was pouring snot, her eyes were red as a Tregaryn's, and every few minutes she was hit with a racking cough that doubled her over, clutching her aching stomach.

"There's really nothing you can take for this?" Narita asked, bewildered.

"I've taken everything." Cough, cough, hack up a lung. Or at least it sounded that way. "This cold is resistant."

It couldn't be resistant enough to make it past Narita's protections, could it? A new mutation? Narita had been torn between the desire to nurse her girlfriend back to health, and the need to flee the apartment, before this terror got her too. Love won out over self-interest, just barely. Well, love and trust in the genetic invulnerability that had blessed her for two decades. She brought Amara a few cup of tea, and pulled the blankets up around her on the couch. Narita rested one hand on her forehead—unscientific, she knew, and yet she couldn't help trusting the aeons-old test. No fever, thankfully. Nothing to do, it seemed, but ride this out.

She had offered, once, to pay for Amara to have some genetic work done. Narita couldn't actually afford that yet, especially since modding adults was so much more expensive than modding sperm, eggs, and blastocysts, but she could talk her mother into it. Probably. At least a little bit—some basic mods to avoid life-threatening diseases, at least. It terrified Narita, knowing that Amara could be carried off by something as simple as the flu. So she had offered to pay for the mods, the same way she'd offered to pay for their celebratory graduation night out the previous month. But Amara had refused, quietly but firmly. She also refused to explain why; Narita still didn't know whether Amara's objections had to do with money, or religion, or something else entirely.

They'd been dating for less than a year—maybe Amara would change her mind down the road. In several years, Narita would be a doctor, making enough money of her own to pay for the procedures; she couldn't touch her inheritance until she was thirty, but she wouldn't need to. She could talk Amara into it then, if they were still together. And she wanted them to stay together, she did. Narita still couldn't explain it to her friends—in fact, she barely saw most of her old friends, these days. It wasn't comfortable, spending time with them and with Amara together. But she didn't need them. All she wanted was Amara, all the time.

Even now—Amara was repulsive in this moment. *Ugly*. And

yet her weakness engendered a strange protectiveness in Narita. At this impossible moment, desire rose up alongside revulsion, and Narita wanted nothing more than to kiss Amara speechless. She doubted her girlfriend would take kindly to any advances right now, though. So instead, Narita paced back and forth in the apartment that seemed suddenly too small, fighting a rising tide of desire and frustration.

It would be another year before Narita asked Amara to partner, to have a child with her, but she had spent nine years looking back, analyzing their relationship. Chieri said it was that night, when Amara was so sick, that Narita had decided she wanted to spend her life with her. Chieri was usually right about such things. It was part of her job.

Her steps hadn't taken her home, to her apartment full of guests. Something in the back of her brain had turned her around, and now she was headed down Atrena, towards Iskander Road. Narita had ended up on the edge of the Warren, which was a stupid place to be tonight, and she was too smart to be so stupid. There was only one reason to be down here, a reason that had nothing to do with buying fresh fruits and vegetables, and what were the odds that Chieri would be out on a night like tonight anyway? Sitting in her window with her dark hair falling loose, long legs hanging over the side, wrapped in a see-through slip that was designed to tear off with a fingertip of pressure—oh, Narita remembered the first time she'd seen Chieri sitting there, the first time she'd followed a beckoning finger inside. Nine years ago, raw and aching. It had been worth a week's salary to bury herself in Chieri's body for a night and forget, forget the woman who had rejected her. The woman who had finally come back.

Tonight, her body didn't feel like her own anymore. Not since Amara walked in her door, and the sudden desire flared through her. As if the past ten years hadn't happened, as if they were still twenty, young and ignorant and bursting with life. Amara looked different now—older, more tired. Wrinkles at the corners of her eyes already; Narita wouldn't wrinkle for decades to come, not if her parents and the gene specialists had done their job right. Narita knew that she must look like a ghost of the past to Amara, virtually unchanged since the day she'd walked away, and perhaps it was petty of her to be pleased by that. Good—let Amara look old and haggard, let her be jealous of how good Narita still looked! And if all Narita wanted to do was wrap her ex-girlfriend in her arms and drag her off to bed—well, she didn't have to let Amara know it.

While Narita had busied herself helping as best she could with the birth of Jequith's child, Amara had huddled in a chair. There was too much chaos in those moments for them to talk, and Narita was glad for the distraction. As soon as the new family was settled, warm and clean and wrapped up entirely in each other, Narita had grabbed her mesh shopping bag and headed out the door. Oh, they could have managed on what was in the pantry, and fine, maybe that would have been smarter, on a night like tonight. The truth was that if she stayed in the apartment, she would have to talk to Amara, and that was one thing she didn't want to do. She didn't even want to see her face. Except she did, she did—Narita wanted to trace every line, every wrinkle on that face with her fingertips— and that was the problem, and that was why she was out the door on this strangely freezing night, shivering and stomping her way down the road. To the market, and then here.

There was the house, so discreet, tucked back from the street like all the others on Iskander Road, front gardens carefully tended, walls well-dressed in sober, rich colors. If you didn't know better, you would assume doctors lived here, or businessfolk. If you didn't see the sacred star that hung from each door, seven-pointed and shining gently in the night. A different branch of Hinduism than the one Amara's family followed—Chieri would say, an older one. There were a thousand tributaries from that stream, some of which you could barely call Hinduism at all, and if one was older than the other, only the scholars bothered to argue about it now. The sacred star promised music and dance, comfort and ecstasy, what-

ever your heart most needed, offered to you by the devadasis, in
the service of their gods.

Offered for a price, of course—salvation doesn't come for free,
and the temple and its grounds were in endless need of attention.
But Narita would never say Chieri didn't earn her pay, not that first
night, nor all the ones after. Three thousand years the devadasis
had been offering their worship, first on old Earth, and then here;
they'd had plenty of time to refine their craft into something quite
astonishing. When you visited a devadasi, ecstasy was guaran-
teed—at least for a few hours.

She and Chieri had become friends, eventually. Friends enough
that Chieri could ask her, under cover of darkness in the early
hours of the morning, why Narita kept coming back, month after
month and year after year; it wasn't as if she needed to pay for
love. Narita kissed Chieri's mouth closed, rather than give her the
real answer—that it was better to pay for it. Safer. This way, no
one's heart was at risk. No one could be abandoned and betrayed.

Chieri's windows were closed tonight, and the star on her door
was dark. She wasn't open for business, or she was already otherwise occupied. Narita should leave her alone, but instead, she
found herself standing in front of the door, banging on it. *Bang!*
Bang! Bang! An unsettling echo of earlier events. How many people
tonight were running from one door to another, searching for
comfort in the encroaching dark?

God, it was cold. And raining again, bitter rain that slanted through
the night with increasing force. No answer at the door, and finally,
Narita had to turn away, admit that there was nothing here for her,
no help. She would have to go back. And in that turning, she saw
them. Amara, on the road behind her—what was she doing here?
Had she followed Narita all this way? Narita's heart, irritatingly,
thumped. And ahead, at the cross street, Chieri, inhumanly beautiful as always, wrapped in a thick, warm cloak. And finally, further
up the road, a strange saurian—short and heavy and dressed in a
campus guard uniform. All of them converging on her. One, two,

three breaths, and they were upon her, meeting at Chieri's doorstep. Narita didn't know what to say to any of them. Thankfully, Chieri took care of that for her.

"Well," she said, looking around at the small, silent circle. "I suppose you're wondering why I've called you all here tonight." It was said dryly enough, but no one laughed, or even smiled. Not tonight. Chieri shrugged. "You'd better come inside."

In the House of God

Amara followed the others inside the star-marked house—the lizard-man, Narita, and the sacred dancer. She kept her distance, a few feet behind, and by the time she crossed the threshold, they were already through the foyer and had entered a room on the far side. Which was just as well, because Amara took one step inside, letting the door swing shut behind her, and then stopped, stunned.

The interior was beautiful. That was the only word for it. Well, that and luxurious, impressive, glorious, expensive. Maybe expensive most of all, because even though every element—the floors, the walls, the curving staircase—was in impeccably good taste, the materials used were higher quality than Amara had ever seen outside a holo. Imported marble, rare woods, shining platinum. Her entire bedroom would fit in this space, with room to spare—and this was just the foyer. It wasn't what she'd expected, from a devadasi's home. She hadn't really known what to expect.

Amara had entered knowing what kind of house this was, trying to be respectful, despite the pit of jealousy churning in her stomach. The woman's profession was holy, even if it wasn't Amara's own religion. Not that Amara had much of a religion anymore—she kept searching, reading, studying, even after she'd finished at university. But the belief that had seemed so easy as a child had died the day her father left; all her searching hadn't revived it. Her parents would never have entered a house like this, but they had always insisted on the importance of respecting others' religious traditions. *We all come to God in different ways, rasathi,* her mother had said. Well, Uma used to say that. In the old days, before Amara's father had left them.

As a teen, Amara had found her parents' broad-mindedness frustrating. *All the ways can't be the right way,* she had insisted. *Some of them contradict each other.* Her parents would just look at each other and laugh in that annoying way they had, as if they were reading each others' minds. An intimacy so sweet and powerful, it left everybody else out. Sometimes, Amara felt like she could *feel* her spine stiffening in sheer irritation.

If she had known then that just a few years later, her father would walk away, would she have treasured that parental closeness? Not that she could have possibly predicted that Dayan would, on Amara's acceptance to university, announce that he was done as householder and father, free to go out into the wilderness and seek God. None of them saw that coming—not even, to his credit, Dayan himself. She had to believe that. That sometimes lives were shattered by bolts that arrived unexpectedly, falling from a clear blue sky.

A dozen years ago, that night. Sitting on the hall stairs, listening to her parents' low voices, a room away.

"Why *now*, kunju? Her mother, pleading. "You still have work to do at the temple, and after that, you will have many years to enjoy as retiree, to spend with your children, your grandchildren." Amara's elder sisters already had prodigious broods, six and seven children each, respectively. "It is not *time* to take up the renunciate's path. Not yet."

Her father's voice was thick. "Uma, I am sorry, believe me. If I could take you and the children with me, I would. But my heart tells me that I must have solitude to find the path."

Her mother was silent for a long time, exhausted by the hours of struggle. Amara and her sisters had been present for much of it, the long day's arguments. With nightfall, her sisters had gone home, and Amara had gone upstairs. She had tried to sleep. But grief burned in her chest, and she eventually crept down the stairs again, to sit on the bottom step and, like a small child, try to over-hear her parents' conversation.

Uma said, finally, "Do you have to go so *far*?" The pain in her voice could break a daughter's heart.

Amara had wondered about this too. There were retreats on-world, many of them. There were many religions that recommended time away from the cares of the everyday world, and a seeker could choose from ashrams in field and forest, over and under sea, in fertile jungle or desolate desert. Even on a solitary mountaintop, if you so desired. You could go, for a time, and then come home. You could have visitors.

Very few made Dayan's choice. To go up, up, up to the stars, sealed in a tiny tin box, hooked up to machines and kept alive for weeks, months, years at a time. So that there was nothing to do, nothing one could do, except contemplate the empty universe, the face of God.

"I have very far to go, my dear," was all her husband said in reply.

Amara knew, when she heard him say those words, that it didn't matter what else her mother said that night. Dayan was going, and Uma was going to let him.

Maybe that was why Amara had married Rajiv. There were many reasons. The most obvious was because Amara was angry. She couldn't marry the woman she wanted, not without crossing lines no one in her family had ever crossed. She knew how her mother would feel, if Amara married a woman from one of *those* families. Uma was the pandit's wife, co-leader of their community, enmeshed in her people's everyday lives and difficulties. She would never be comfortable with Narita's people, with their wealth and oh-so-considered kindness. If Amara married Narita, she would be leaving her own world and entering another. Leaving her mother behind. Her father had done that to Uma already; Amara couldn't be the one to break her mother's heart again.

So she was angry. Twenty years old, that anger turned into spite. Amara asked Uma to arrange her marriage, and then married the right kind of man—not rich, but with a steady job. Educated, intelligent, someone's who'd worked hard and made a solid place for himself in the world. The kind of man her mother approved of. But, angry, Amara made the wrong kind of marriage. Uma was shocked by Amara's decision to pledge life marriage, such a heedless, immoderate choice. No one in their family had pledged life marriage in generations—not since her many-great grandparents had left Earth in their own tiny metal ship. It was the sort of thing adolescents might dream about, viewing historical holovids, but no one actually did anymore. Life marriage was as foolish as not keeping your own credit account, or giving up your own name. Archaic, romantic, ridiculous.

Why had she done it? Amara didn't really know. Maybe because she'd always loved old things, old ways. Maybe because Amara wanted what her parents had had, once upon a time. Most likely, she'd harassed Rajiv into agreeing to life marriage so she could pretend that they really were bound forever. Soulmates. She'd married him for life, so that her husband would never leave her.

After announcing his intentions, her father had waited two more months, until the end of his sixth five-year term of marriage. Thirty years, three daughters, thirteen grandchildren. And then Dayan had simply not renewed his marriage, left his wife to lead their congregation, dissolved all his personal savings to pay for the ship, and walked away from them all. Flew.

It had all seemed to make sense at the time, when she had gone to her mother and asked to have her marriage arranged, had insisted on a life marriage. But now, all those reasons dissipated like dust on the breeze. Maybe the truth was simpler; Amara had run away from Narita because she was afraid. Had run straight to Rajiv and locked herself into that marriage, strapped as tightly as her father in his little tin ship. Tighter. Because her father had broken his promises—not explicit vows of marriage, perhaps, but implicit promises. *I love you now, and tomorrow, and all the days after.* He had broken his promises to his wife, his daughters, and so Amara couldn't break a promise. Not ever. She had sworn life marriage, and trapped herself. Mistake piled on mistake; calamity leading to catastrophe. An endless empty desolation.

Until war was declared, and missiles streaked overhead, and Rajiv confessed that he had shattered the bonds of their marriage.

The tubes that had been inserted into her arteries and veins, binding her in place, were now ripped out and dripping strange fluids. Oh, she wasn't making sense, not even in her own head, but did that matter on a night like this? Amara was free, she could go anywhere. She had nowhere to go.

Her father's ship was still up there, somewhere in the space between the stars, searching for god. Amara checked in on the news, as she'd been doing periodically, obsessively, since the announcement came—still quiet up there, nothing more since that first rocket, which they were now saying had been ground-based. So far, there were no explosions in space, and even if there were, it was vanishingly unlikely that a missile would happen across his particular point in space. Unlikely, but possible. Should she worry for her father? Should she grieve?

Amara shook her head, casting away ragged memories. She had enough to worry about now, in this moment—no need to dwell on the wounds of the past. In this room, envy joined jealousy in the battle for her heart; it wasn't fair, that Amara had to compete with all this splendor. If the woman's house was this beautiful, what must she be like? Amara had avoided looking at the woman. But now, against her will, she was imagining Narita here. Had her ex-girlfriend lain naked on the Persian rug in the foyer, pale brown skin against a thousand shades of red? The rug looked ancient, as if it had come all the way from old Earth, after being woven by skilled human hands. Amara was sure it hadn't just been extruded from the assembler last week.

The others were already sitting down in the living room, but Amara could not bring herself to cross the hall towards them. She stood frozen on the antique rug, hating herself. She should have stayed at the apartment. Of course she had known Narita didn't want to talk to her, but Amara couldn't bear to stay with the aliens. She had to deal with occasional aliens at work, but at work they came, shuffled up in the queue, filled out their forms, and shuffled away again. And the air filters at work were good.

It was different being alone with them, trapped in a tiny apartment, the acrid scent of them filling the place. It didn't help that the neuter's hand was never far from that sharp carving knife it wore. Amara's skin was crawling within moments of Narita's departure for the market, even though she knew she should be more open-minded, more accepting. She wanted to be better. But when the neuter squatted near its child and squirted a stream of goo from its mouth over the child's skin, that was just too much.

Amara didn't know what it was doing, and she didn't care—she had bolted out the door, swallowing hard to keep the last sad remnants of her dinner in her stomach. She'd given praise to all the gods that she could still see Narita striding with her long legs down the street, two blocks away already and almost out of sight. She'd followed Narita down a maze of streets, to the market and then down Iskander Road, wondering where she was going. Amara had never come down this way before; it wasn't the sort of place her people went. She'd never have expected Narita to come to a place like this. How long had Narita been seeing this woman? Was it purely a business relationship, or something more?

She hadn't really expected Narita to be waiting for her, when Amara fled her house, her marriage. Narita could have easily found a partner by now, contracted, had children. Amara wasn't stupid; she *knew* that. But she had hoped that Narita might have forgiven her, at least, in the nine intervening years. That they could be friends. And if she *were* available they might have a chance—but the way Narita had avoided even meeting her eyes since Amara's arrival at her door suggested otherwise.

There was a hole in her heart, and her blood was gushing out, pooling around her, a sea of crimson soaking into the red rug. Over-dramatic, over-intense, that was what her husband had always called her. How would he know? Rajiv was too cold and calculating to have a heart.

She fought the urge to just sink to the ancient rug and cry, overwhelmed by a wave of bitterness and despair. Amara wrapped her arms around herself, fingers digging into chilled flesh, as if the pain might anchor her here, carry her to a new reality. But she couldn't fall to the floor; she couldn't even stand on this rug forever. For a moment, Amara considered just turning around and walking out the door. She could go anywhere. But then Narita came to the doorway and beckoned. *Come here.* And Amara went.

Amara hesitated in the doorway, but finally, not knowing what else to do, she came fully into the room and sank down onto a cushion, intensely conscious of her grubby, wet clothes. Low velvet-covered seats in jewel tones surrounded a silvered tea table, and the woman was already pouring tea from a graceful glass vessel. How had she kept the water hot while she was out? But ah, there in the corner, a small fire burned merrily in a hearth, and a large kettle hung above it. Safe enough to leave, for a little while. Clever. The neroli tea scent was strong, and incense smoked in the hearth as well. Amara felt dizzy, flushed. What a long night it had been.

"Chieri, do we really have time for tea?" the security guard asked.

The woman—Chieri—smiled gently. "Gaurav, my dear—if we don't take time for tea now, then when? Her voice was low and melodious; she almost sounded as if she were singing when she spoke. They had engineered even that. Had her parents known what she would become, that they had made her so painfully lovely? Amara blinked, and blinked again, trying to clear away the shining halo from her eyes. Chieri seemed to glow, like a holo, or a goddess.

She was tall, taller than anyone else in the room, and rich with curves barely restrained by her sari. A sari that, by the look of it, cost more than Amara and her husband together had earned in a month. But you almost didn't notice it, because Chieri's body, her face, were so perfect. Inhuman, the kind of beauty that stole your breath. Unfair. Amara's heart was pounding, and sweat beaded on her upper lip. She surreptitiously wiped it away, feeling as crass and young as a schoolgirl. Simultaneously angry and aroused. What was she doing here, in this company?

They would have curved together in the night, arms entwined, lips hot against each other. Narita and Chieri, Chieri and Narita. Amara could *see* the slick bodies moving in a perfect dance, as if choreographed. Breasts as firm and taut as they'd been ten years before, and would be ten years to come. Not a wrinkle, not a line, and in that moment, Amara wanted to dig her nails into her own face and rip it apart. Her nose was too big, her eyes too small. There were surgeries for that, to make her almost as beautiful as these two. But even if she could have afforded the surgeries, each cut would leave a scar. Invisible to the eye, but she would always know they were there. And her mother would never forgive her.

Chieri poured a cup of tea, gracefully, of course. "We must make time for what small civilities we have left. After all, the world may be ending."

"You don't believe that," Narita snapped. "This war won't touch most of the humans on the planet. They'll just go on with their daily lives, barely thinking about it." She glanced at Amara then, a sharp, cutting glance. Was that comment directed at her? Of course it was. Narita had always said Amara was too self-in-volved, that she didn't pay enough attention to galactic politics. At twenty, Amara had thought it wiser to find her own center, her straight path, before meddling in the outside world. But somehow, over the years, she had lost her center too. And now the world—the universe—was falling apart.

"You think the people aren't paying attention, Narita? Truly?" Chieri shook her head. "They may want to ignore the war, they may manage to push it to the bottom of their minds. But as long as the fighting continues, it will always be present in their hearts." She laughed, though there was no real humor in the sound. "It's already been a busy night; I expect I and my fellow celebrants will continue busy for the duration."

Narita bit her lip, as if she were unhappy with that thought. Amara felt her chest tighten further, painfully—how close *were* they? Had it started as work for hire, but then turned into some-thing more? Did Narita love this woman?

Chieri shifted in her chair, leaning forward to hand Narita her tea. Their fingertips touched, and Chieri's hair swung low and loose, brushing their hands in a fall of midnight. How could anyone resist this goddess? The scent of her, dark and musky, was laced with pheromones—that must be why Amara's own thighs were trembling, the space between them wet. That scent made it almost impossible to think. If Chieri held out a hand to Amara, would she go to her too?

Chieri turned to look at Amara then, the first time their eyes had met since Amara's arrival. Chieri smiled, a smile as sweet as starry jasmine. Her beauty pierced Amara like a spear, and in that moment, she could feel her heart tumbling in her chest, falling over itself with eagerness. Chieri's smile offered solace to all Amara's griefs. It would be so easy to slide off her chair, to crawl across the lush rug and lay her weary head on Chieri's knee. A promise of release, of ecstasy. Was this what her father sought, out among the stars?

A pathway to the gods, the holy dancers were said to be. Their song along was a miracle, sought after by kings for generation upon generation. Their dance was renowned across the universe. And if you were lucky enough to be graced with something more… Amara had tried her parents' paths of discipline, ascetic purity, fidelity. What had they gotten her? Maybe license was a better answer. Chieri's eyes glowed in the firelight, and her skin begged to be touched, caressed. Amara could glory in its silken splendor, drown in a sea of midnight desire.

But then Chieri said, breaking the spell, "And this—oh, I know who this must be. Amara, your lost love."

Narita had told this woman about her? Had told her enough that Chieri could recognize her on a few minutes' acquaintance. Amara's heart thumped, seemingly loud enough for everyone to hear, and she found herself, involuntarily, on her feet. *What* had Chieri called her? What did it mean, that Narita would speak of her, and of love, to this woman? Amara was poised on the balls of her feet. Ready to flee. Ready to fall.

Narita frowned and shook her head, avoiding Amara's eyes. "This isn't the time." Amara felt her heart crash back into her chest, and then sink, a fallen star, cold as empty space, settling in the pit of her stomach. She didn't belong here. Amara took two steps to the doorway and leaned against the frame. A storm was battering its way inside her body, stealing the strength from her muscles and bones. She would fall down without the wall to prop her up.

The guard, Gaurav, said in a rough voice, "I agree. This is no time to speak of love. Chieri, why did you call me here?"

She spread graceful hands. "I didn't know who else to call. Your partner Kris was always so kind to me, so generous."

"I am not Kris," Gaurav said stiffly.

The prostitute bit her lip. "I know you're not Kris—but I needed someone with power, authority. Someone I could trust." She looked for the first time since their arrival uncertain, almost frightened. "I don't know what to do now; maybe you can help. There was a worshipper here earlier. I was out looking for him when you arrived—he was so intoxicated when he left that I wasn't sure he would make it more than a block away. But he's gone."

Gaurav frowned, "Did you give him something?" Sounding very much like a policeman. If only Amara could apply to him for help. *Officer, I seem to have lost something. My path, my life, my heart.*

Chieri frowned. "Drugged devotees are risky for those in my profession; I try to avoid them. Whatever was wrong with him, he arrived that way. I'm not sure what he was on, exactly. Something I haven't seen before, that made him happy, almost giddy. Although under that was a river of grief. He was completely lacking in inhibitions, which I'm guessing is why he made his way here—apparently, I'm the first whore he's ever visited."

Narita winced, and said, "You know I don't like it when you call yourself that?"

Chieri raised a perfect eyebrow. "But my dear, it's accurate, in its own way, as you well know. And it was the word he used."

"Still," Narita said. Amara swallowed down everything she could have said.

Chieri shrugged and went on. "His name was Mikash. I danced for him, shared his bed. Afterwards, when we resting, he said he was responsible for the missile that hit the Warren. At least I think that's what he was saying—I could barely understand him, his speech was so confused. And his accent was thick; he was from the backcountry, one of the distant agricultural districts."

Narita was frowning, leaning forward, but she said nothing. Amara was sure Narita was angry, though she wouldn't show it; that was the rocket that had injured Narita's friends, almost killed their baby.

The lizard-man frowned. "You should have called the campus guard central. If he was responsible for the earlier attack, then we need to mobilize the authorities to find him."

"No, you don't understand," Chieri said, her voice rising. "It was Mikash's fault; he had set off one missile, too early. Apparently, the men he was with have many, many more, and are just waiting for sunrise. I'm not sure why—I'm not sure he knew either. He was very confused, and I got the impression that he hadn't been told much. But he was sure of one thing—whomever he'd been working for, they were planning to completely wipe out the Warren, and everyone in it."

Narita asked, curiously, "And you believe him? A drugged-out yokel with delusions of grandeur?" Amara agreed that it seemed unlikely; wasn't it more logical that some backcountry boy had come to the city to visit a devadasi with a year's salary in his pocket, had gotten scared, bought some drugs to help him through it, and then made up a story that he thought would impress a girl?

Chieri hesitated before speaking, looking around at their faces. Then she seemed to make a decision, and said, quietly, "We don't usually reveal this; I'm sure you can understand why. But many of the devadasis are mildly empathic. It is useful in our line of work, and when we can, we breed for it. I am stronger than most, and I am fairly sure—whatever is actually going on, Mikash *believed* he was telling the absolute truth."

Amara was startled, though when she thought about it, not actually all that surprised. There were telepathic species among the non-humans, and occasional empaths and telepaths even among humans. Though she'd never heard of a community of them, Chieri's revelation made a certain sense. Narita was silent, although she drew her body back further onto the couch, as if she were pulling away from the devadasi. It might be disturbing, after the fact, to learn that your lover knew you more intimately than you had thought. Amara tried not to feel too happy at that thought. Chieri glanced at Narita, and then turned back to Gaurav.

Gaurav rose to his feet, one hand drifting closer to his holstered weapon. "If this is true, I have to tell my captain; I'm going to need you to come with me."

Chieri bit her lip and then asked, "Can you trust him?"

Gaurav opened his mouth as if to say *of course*—and then stopped, mouth open. He froze for a long moment there, struggle visible even on his scaly face. And then he admitted, "Maybe not. Captain Raj would take my report—and then might just decide to do nothing about it. He might think it was a convenient way to solve a problem."

"The Devadasi Council believes the government is involved in these attacks," Chieri said quietly. "I *cannot* put myself into official hands. I didn't know who to trust; that's why I called you. And I will not reveal our empathic abilities—not now, when the Humans First groups are stoking fears about even innocuous modifications. If people thought we could read their minds—well, not only might they stop visiting us out of fear, that fear could easily turn into rage and violence. If you force me to go to to your captain, I will have to deny all of this."

Chieri turned them, spreading her hands wide, including them all in her desperate desire. Amara almost fell off her chair at the force of it, the *need* to help this poor woman, to do whatever it would take to make her happy. Pheromones? Was she a projective empath too? Or was this just a helpless woman's desperation, on this terrible night?

Chieri pleaded, "Please, all of you—can you do anything? We only have a few hours, and I—I don't know what to do." She wrapped her arms around herself, swaying slightly. "If this is real, if they succeed—a lot of people in the Warren will die. And that might be just the beginning."

All Amara wanted was to leave the house of this woman, dancer, priestess. Whore. But then the words Chieri had said penetrated. Many more missiles. *Completely wipe out theWarren.* She didn't know anyone who lived there. But that didn't matter, did it? It would be mass murder, and no matter what Amara thought about aliens—or humods, for that matter—killing them was wrong. That part of the path was clear enough. If her parents were here, she knew what they would do—take charge, organize the community, make a plan. She had seen it so many times growing up, watched her parents mobilize people in response to a crisis—a food shortage, a fire, an illness that swept through the community. She and her sisters had helped—making the calls, explaining the problem, arguing out the details of the plan.

It was a blessed relief, in the midst of everything, to finally know what to do.

She straightened up, away from the supporting doorframe. Amara opened her mouth, for the first time since she'd arrived. The first time in hours, actually, since she'd knocked on Narita's door. Amara opened her mouth and said the words, knowing the price they would exact. "I want to help."

This damnable night wasn't over yet.

Seeking Clarity

Chieri longed to go to her rooftop chambers, to immerse herself in the rituals that would bring her peace. The tea ceremony had helped a little, even in abbreviated form, but tonight she needed more. Needed to kneel on the raw slate, wrap the cords around her arms, tilt her head back and gaze up, through the stained glass star on her ceiling, to the real stars beyond. Acera lo siqueriel, diantha re zarim. Even now, surrounded by people, she felt the chant bubbling in her throat, longing to be released, and it took all her strength to restrain it. Chieri's toes curled into the plush fibers of the rug; her thighs tensed, gripping the silken cushion of her chair. The woman was talking. Chieri had delivered her message, passed along the information. She didn't know what else to do. Rasti re sempervens, acera lo acera re acera everá!

Amara said, "All right. It's almost one now. Sunrise is at—" a pause, while Amara checked the net—"7:12 a.m. So we have six hours." She swallowed hard. "Six hours to stop a bunch of maniacs armed with missiles, who are planning wholesale slaughter. Hells." Amara fell silent, and the silence grew, gathering weight in the dimly-lit room. No one seemed to want to speak next. Chieri couldn't blame them.

She slipped back in time. Six hours until sunrise on the longest night of her life, the night she kept vigil before taking her final vows, dedicating her life to the gods. Her creche-parents claimed that at thirty, Chieri was too young to make such a commitment, even though they had been training her for this holy work from birth. From before birth. Even now, while she knelt naked in the garden on the night of dedication, her first-mother sat beside her, cross-legged on a wrought iron bench. Karista had dressed in her favorite sari, the silks a riot of shimmering color, as if she meant to tempt her daughter with all the pleasures of the world.

"It's not easy, the life of a devadasi. I know that better than anyone. Some days it's a miracle that our creche-group survives; jealousies rise up, and threaten to tear us apart. Chieri, kunju, please think. There are so many other, easier paths to follow. You could become a doctor instead," Karista offered. "You have the hands of a surgeon."

Cutting people open, slicing through their flesh and guts? There was a need for such work, Chieri knew, but the thought of it repulsed her; it would be as bad as eating meat. Worse. She kept her silence, not bothering to dignify her mother's suggestion with a response. Strictly speaking, there was no requirement that Chieri maintain silence all night, but she had thought it would add to the ritual, to the holiness of it. Although it was impossible to feel the presence of the gods with her mother here, picking at her.

Maybe that was Karista's goal, to intervene between her daughter and the gods. But why, when it was Karista's own path that Chieri was trying to follow? Did her mother think she wasn't good enough, strong enough? Or was Karista jealous of her daughter, wanting to keep the gods to herself? It hurt, that moment of believing her mother could be so cruel. It had almost been enough to break her resolve. But there was too much at stake for Chieri to give up so easily. She took a deep breath, and held firm.

Gaurav's voice broke the silence, snapping Chieri back to the present. He was frowning. "Why would they wait for sunrise? Why not just set the missiles off now?"

Narita suggested, "Better publicity? Or they're waiting for someone higher up to arrive? Or maybe whatever tech they're using takes time to implement?"

Amara shook her head. "There are too many possibilities, and it doesn't matter anyway. We can't waste time trying to figure out their motives—we need to focus on stopping them. Agreed?"

Gaurav looked like he wanted to argue, but after a moment, he nodded. Chieri was sure that he would keep puzzling at it, though—he wouldn't be able to help himself. She could feel it in him, the low-level empathy her parents had gifted her with whispering his needs to her, under her skin. Gaurav needed answers, Narita needed love, or the memory of it at least, Amara needed something worthwhile to do. They all needed sex—it had been some time for each of them—although it wasn't foremost in their minds at the moment. They were practically shouting their needs, the air thick with their thoughts—this was why Chieri only took one worshipper at a time. It was too hard to focus with three of them in the room, their needs hammering at her. And tonight, everyone's emotions were heightened, even her own. She needed the ritual to find herself again. *Acera lo, acera re.*

"All right," Amara continued. "Now, catalogue our information. Do we know where they are?"

They turned to Chieri, and she took a focusing breath, trying to remember what the boy, Mikash, had said. Her head hurt; it pounded, making it hard to think. It was as if something didn't want her to think, was drawing her back to that night, so many years ago.

"Or you could open a flower shop. Your garden is coming along very nicely." Her mother had bent her head, burying her nose in a spray of blue jasmine that wound its way along the back of the garden bench.

That was a bit more enticing—Chieri enjoyed the hours she spent digging and snipping and weeding. She took pleasure in the process of shaping the garden to best effect, encouraging healthy growth, ruthlessly eliminating pests and blight. It was not so different from the work she did with people—but truthfully, much less satisfying. Because for all her efforts, in the end, the plants were just plants. At their very best, they were still so much less than the most twisted person's soul. Even when people were battered or broken, they carried a core of light within them. And when Chieri touched them, with hands and mouth and sacred yoni, she could, if for only a moment, set them free. In that moment, a person glowed like fire. Chieri couldn't give up that glory just to work with plants. *Acera re, acera lo, tempe saldi everá.*

"Chieri?" Narita leaned forward, put her hand on Chieri's arm. Narita was warm, almost feverish. Chieri wanted to pull her close, drop kisses on that fevered brow. But the concern—no, the fear— in Narita's face steadied her. They had asked her a question, hadn't they? Where was Mikash, the boy?

"He didn't say a place, exactly." He had been making so little sense, and at first, she hadn't even been trying to listen. Chieri had focused on what her body was conveying, what she could read of his exhilaration, his anxiety. "He had driven the missile some-where, on a test run? That was when he set it off, by mistake."

Gaurav was nodding. "Yes, they tracked the path back to where the rocket launched, and found an abandoned truck there. That part of the story makes sense."

Narita said, "I don't see anything about a truck on the net."

"They haven't released that information to the public yet," Gaurav said, impatiently. "Go on, Chieri. What else?"

She said, slowly, "I think he talked about tunnels, and maybe a door?" That hadn't been words, actually, more of a picture. Some-times her empathy slid almost over into telepathy; Chieri would get flashes of images sometimes from the worshippers. That wasn't anything she cared to advertise, though—she had already told them too much, far more than the Council would approve of, if they knew. Let these three believe the boy had said the words. "Yes—a huge wood-and-metal door."

Narita bit her lip. "I think I know where that must be. The sci-ence complex has a shielded set of tunnels underneath it, almost a maze. And at the center of the labyrinth is one of the oldest build-ings on campus. They brought it from Earth, rebuilt it here, piece by piece. Those doors are a thousand years old."

Gaurav was nodding. "The students call it Kali's Gate."

"Why?" Amara asked.

Narita answered, "Some long-gone artist shaped intricate patterns, depicting the goddess at war, out of forged iron. It's beautiful—you would like it." She said that last reluctantly, as if she didn't want to admit to even that much between them, that she would know what Amara would like. Chieri wondered how long Narita would fight the pull she could feel between the two of them. Maybe forever. People could be stubborn that way.

Gaurav frowned. "It's strong, and worse, it's going to be fucking impossible to get to it. It's a maze to get in there. A series of underground tunnels, with blast doors at various points, all controlled by a complex security system. A lot of people have access to the blast doors, since there are classrooms behind them, but Kali's Gate guards the deepest labs."

Narita continued, "Normally, all the blast doors are slid open, and the students wander freely, right up to the Gate—that's how I've seen it. But in case of emergency, they all slam shut to protect the computer and science labs on the lower levels."

Gaurav said grimly, "I'm pretty sure tonight counts as an emergency; the blast doors, Kali's Gate, and the labs behind it will be locked down tight. If this Mikash is right, whomever's behind this picked a smart place to work from."

"But there aren't any missiles down there," Narita said, frowning.

Gaurav shook his head. "No. But there's a serious computer lab, one of the best on the planet. If you were good enough, you might be able to hack into some of the private weapons research labs from there. And then they must have people on the ground, backcountry boys like Mikash, moving the missiles so they can't be tracked? Sacrificial goats in case they get caught. I'm betting it's something like that. The question is, how did they get access? Not even faculty can get in there; only senior administrators should have biometric access to that room."

Amara said, impatiently, "Irrelevant. The question is, how do *we* get access to that room?"

Chieri had no idea. And now the river was tugging at her again, pulling back to the past, even more strongly. Why was she fighting it? Surely that night was better than this? And she had trained her whole life to listen to such impulses—sometimes, they were the voice of the gods, speaking through her. If they wanted her to go back, she must go.

Her mother leaned forward, hands clasped in her sari silks, her eyes brightly intent. "You could be a dancer. A secular dancer—we gave you the body for it, and you've practiced the skills. You could travel the worlds, performing for audiences of thousands or more. Have your work broadcast across the stars, reaching millions. Think of the glory!"

Ah, here was a real temptation, Chieri admitted in the privacy of her mind. It did frustrate her that her best work was often done with just one person to appreciate it. There were some devadasis, she knew, who had their worshippers sign releases, so that they could record and broadcast the experience. They could get rich with such practices, and would argue that it was entirely in keeping with their holy duties, a way of reaching a broader community.

But such recordings had always seemed distateful to Chieri, a perversion of their sacred labor. If their bodies and dancing were pathways to the gods, then was that not a most intimate experience? One to be experienced and shared in the privacy of your home, with at most a few chosen souls, not broadcast for the worlds to see and hear. Even leaving privacy concerns aside—visuals and auditory sensations weren't enough. Without the body and its kinetic experience to ground you, you risked losing touch with what was truly important. The pulsebeat that opened you up, a stairway straight to the heavens.

She could feel it now, finally, thrumming through her. *Ace re alla than. Thi thi thay, thi thi thay.* From the soles of her feet to her trembling thighs, from her belly to breasts and up and up. As if a pulse of power was shooting straight through her, reaching from the ground to the open sky and naked stars above. *Acero la, allaree!*

Her mother could see it too, could feel the energy sparking. Karista sighed, a sigh that seemed composed of equal parts regret and relief, and rose gracefully to her feet. She bent her head and dropped a kiss on her daughter's forehead, a kiss that caught fire and blazed in the darkness. Then she turned and walked away, down the mossy stone path, leaving a trail of subtle jasmine behind her. Leaving her daughter's body effervescent, in an endless, glorious night.

That night had ended, though, and morning had come. Chieri had taken her vows, and from that point had walked the path that led her here, to this moment of bewilderment, confusion, frustration. They were so small, the four of them, to set against an evil host. And what skills did she have to fight with? Chieri was no computer expert, no soldier. Her body was strong and fast, but unpracticed in the arts of war.

They were all quiet for long, painful moments, until Chieri felt the flash of insight running through Gaurav, like lightning shooting up his curving spine. He said, rising to his feet, "I know someone who can help us. A grad student; she works with weapons systems. Sharp as whip, that's what Kris said. He thought she'd be running the computer lab in a few years."

Amara asked, "So can you reach her?"

He hesitated, and then said, "I have to talk to the captain first."

She frowned. "Even if you don't think he'll help us."

He stared at her, with those unblinking saurian eyes. "You don't understand. I'm a cop. I have to try."

Amara threw up her hands. The frustration was practically boiling off her, but she pushed past it, moving on. "Okay. Okay. Gaurav will try the captain, and if that fails, he'll talk to his computer expert, see if she can get the doors open for us."

Narita snapped, "And then what? We're supposed to go invade some kind of terrorist group, that's trying to set off a bunch of missiles, to slaughter thousands of innocent people. What, the four of us? And what fucking army?"

"We'll think of—" Amara started to say, but Narita cut her off by, unexpectedly, bursting into tears.

They all froze for a second, while Narita buried her face in her hands and sobbed, her shoulders heaving. Chieri was surprised that she hadn't felt this coming—it was as if a switch had flipped in Narita, taking her from irritation to despair in a single moment.

No, that wasn't right. Chieri would like to believe that. But here was the truth; Chieri had buffered herself from them all, had withdrawn as much as she could from the press of their emotions. This was not the way. *Acera lo, risel nithi.* Open, let go. It was hard, so hard, to lower her defenses. But was this not her holy calling? By pulling away, she had failed Narita, who was more than a seeker. Who was a friend.

This was what she had chosen, that night in the garden. No matter how much it hurt, no matter how much she longed to run away. Losing herself in the rituals would bring only false comfort. It would be as much a perversion as any recording of intimacies might be.

So Chieri braced herself with a single sucking breath against the tides, and then opened the floodgates, to feel ah, yes. The despair, howling underneath. Not just in Narita, no. In all of them, fear and grief, confusion and despair, a great frenzied whirlpool that would swallow them down into the night. This was war, battling for their souls.

It was her task, to heal these wounds, but Chieri had never been trained for this. War and death, the weight of a world falling onto shoulders that had been trained to strength—but not enough, surely. *Risei riquel my mothers and fathers. Oh, I am in need of you now.* But they were gone, her creche-parents, lost years ago. And as much as Chieri would have liked to take all three of these lost souls to her bed tonight, to assuage their hurts with flesh and scent, with savoury tastes and long, refreshing draughts of sweetness—there was no time for the deep pleasures, not tonight.

All she could do, all she knew how to do, was dance for them.

Amidst the Shouting

Gaurav fled Chieri's apartment as soon as her dance was over. It had lasted mere minutes, her body stripped bare, curved shapes in the firelight. But it had stroked strange longings in him—desires that he had no time to explore. At least the dance had seemed to bring the weeping female human some peace. Gaurav could almost envy humans their ability to 'cry'—tension choked his throat, and he had to swallow repeatedly before he could speak. He needed to talk to the captain; he wasn't sure of much else, but that part was clear.

He called into the station from his flyer's hardwired line; Gaurav could have called sooner from his internal link, but he'd wanted the privacy of the flyer's curving walls. It was bad enough that there were civilians involved as much as they were—Amara and the others were already rushing off to implement their human schemes. Maybe it was better; they'd be out of harm's way for a little while, at least. "Mitty, I need to talk to the captain."

"Aren't you supposed to be off-duty?" The voice of the desk sergeant came in oddly crackly—systems must be disrupted by the weather somehow, which was getting increasingly turbulent. The trees in the park were whipping their branches fiercely in the wind, and there was an occasional crack of distant thunder overhead. Gaurav hoped he didn't have to do too much flying tonight; the flyers here weren't really designed for anything harsher than the steady pulsing of monsoon rain.

Gaurav asked, "Who's really off-duty tonight?" His shift had ended at eleven, not long after he'd arrived at the site of the explosion earlier. The battered buildings had been swarming with cops, firefighters, and medstaff; all the off-duty people were supposed to go home and rest, so they would be ready for the next shift. But he couldn't have slept, not tonight. So Gaurav had gone back to walking the city streets, weaving in and out of the district, looking for signs of trouble. If Chieri hadn't called him, he'd still be out, walking the night.

Mitty laughed shortly. "Hey, lizard-man, if it were up to me, I'd be at home in my bed tonight, fucking my wife. With the fucking covers up over my head."

"Yeah, well, I'm here. Off the clock, but trying to do some good. And I need to talk to the captain, right now." Mitty was a good guy, but he wasn't used to dealing with real emergencies. None of them were.

"Your funeral, lizard-man." Gaurav could practically hear the sergeant shrugging his shoulders. "Captain Raj is in the foulest of moods."

"Where can I find him?" It might be better to do this in person, rather than trying to convince the captain of the urgency over the phone. As long as the captain was in the city—it was small enough that the flyer could get anywhere in ten minutes.

"At the hospital; you might try the basement morgue. They're still bringing people in."

Gaurav's brow ridges raised. "I thought no one had died?" That had been the one blessing of the single missile—it had knocked down some buildings and torn up the street, but as far as he'd heard, everyone had managed to get out.

"Secondary fallout—two more buildings with shared foundation and systems collapsed. Some bad wounded out of that, and three dead, including one of the firefighters who went in to help. Hell of a night."

"Yeah. Hell of a night." Gaurav cut the connection, and banged the ignition. In moments the flyer was in the air, headed towards the hospital. Knowing that people had died made an already surreal night even stranger; even though he was racing through the sky, it felt as if he were wading through the quicksand bogs of home, moving in slow motion. He'd wasted too much time already; Kris would have known better, would have *done* better.

C'mon, lizard. Move your cold, scaly ass.

He was assaulted by waves of noise as soon he stepped out of the flyer. Hands reached for him, as if he could somehow help them, his uniform a source of momentary solace, before they realized he had nothing for them. Gaurav fought his way through the loud, frenzied crowd outside the hospital, and the anxious horde of relatives and friends in the emergency room.

One little girl, small enough that her feet didn't reach the floor, sat alone. Her eyes were wide and blank, her hair a cloud of black curls around her head, her face and arms a bloody mess of oozing scrapes. Gaurav resisted the urge to go over to her—the room was swarming with people, and surely someone was taking care of her. He had no idea how she felt about saurians, or if she'd ever even seen a non-human in person before. Gaurav didn't want to scare her worse than she was already.

He'd never seen the hospital this busy; most days, the biggest crisis it dealt in were the STDs and surprise pregnancies of young university students who apparently weren't smart enough to use appropriate prophylactics. No one seemed to have any idea where anyone else was, and the hospital staff were clearly harried—one young doctor shouted at a nurse as Gaurav walked past, and the poor man burst into tears.

He finally found the captain in the morgue, as Mitty had suggested, alone, except for the three bodies on the tables.

Raj said softly, as he walked in, "Her name was Velma."

Gaurav said, "I'm sorry, Captain?" Captain Raj was gazing down at the naked woman on the slab in front of him. Young— mid-twenties, perhaps. Dark brown skin, cropped black hair.

Discreetly covered from neck to toes by a sheet, but somehow terribly naked nonetheless. They always looked so cold and vulnerable, the dead. Gaurav hated the morgue.

"Velma deSelby-Bowen. I knew her dad, you know; they lived in my neighborhood, just three apartment buildings down. Satish was so proud that his little girl was going to be a firefighter, just like him. Coached her all the way through the training. I'd see them on the street sometimes, practicing hauling the hose while other kids were learning to drive their first flyers. Velma was a plucky thing—didn't care how ridiculous she looked. And strong. By the end of the summer, she could toss that hose around like it was made of cotton candy, with a heavy pack on her back too. She got some good height on her when puberty hit, and in the end, Velma coasted through the tests. Graduated second in her class at the academy. I bet she saved more than a few lives before the end."

"I'm sure she did, sir." He'd never seen the captain like this—reflective, morose. Gaurav didn't know how to break in with his news, but he had to get the words out. They were burning in his throat.

"I'm glad Satish didn't live to see this. Rigellian flu, you know, three years ago. This is going to break her mother's heart." The captain shook his head fiercely, flecks of ash flying out of his mass of curly grey-black hair as he did. And then he turned, finally, to face Gaurav. "You have something to report?"

Gaurav tried to hold his gaze firm, meeting the captain's intimidating stare. More than a few young cadets had fallen apart while trying to report. But he was better than that; Kris had always believed he was better than that. "Yes, captain. It started when I got a call from Chieri Rasvati. She lives in—"

The captain cut him off. "I know who she is. Your old partner had a weakness for her. That's the sort of thing that gets a good cop in trouble."

How dare the captain say that about Kris? Kris, who had laid down his life for the job, for the people of this city. A flare of rage raced up Gaurav's spine, and he fought the sudden urge to bite the captain's head off. Literally. It wouldn't help matters any. "Yes sir. She'd had a…" he hesitated, not sure how to put it. Client? Congregant? "…a visitor. A kid who said he'd been part of the group that set off the missile."

Raj's gaze sharpened. "Tell me everything. Every fucking detail."

Gaurav did his best, though memory blurred as a wave of exhaustion hit him. It had been a long day, and a long night; his body wanted to curl up in a warm spot and go to sleep. But he fought through it, giving as complete a report as he could. But to no avail.

The captain shook his head at the end of Gaurav's story, interest visibly draining from his face. "Some drugged-out kid says he did it? You're bringing me a report of devadasi pillow talk? There have been dozens of people claiming responsibility for the rocket, and all of them are more credible than that one. Maybe if you had the kid himself… No, I can't spend personnel on it. We're stretched too thin as it is, most of my people are half-asleep, and I can't risk calling directly for government help. Who knows what the fuck we'd get. I know some of the Parliamentarians are big Human First donors."

"But captain—"

Raj sighed. "I'll send it up through official channels, okay? But the lines are jammed with reports, and I'm just a precinct captain. Unless you know someone more important, who can push it to the top of the queue, I'm betting no one's even going to look at my report tonight. Have you seen the net? Did you know the Andressi are threatening to hurl a ship into the Venturi homeworld? No one believes they're crazy enough to try it, or that they would get through if they did, but that's the level of crisis we're dealing with."

Gaurav was shaking with frustration. Send the report up through channels? Was that really all the police would do?

"That's it, Gaurav. Let it go." The captain's voice, inexplicably, gentled. "Your shift was over hours ago. Go home, if your home's still standing. Get some sleep."

"You said my name." Gaurav hadn't meant to say that out loud—he was just so startled. In the years he'd been working at the station, the captain had never called him by name. It was always Lizard-man, or Scaly, or Tailless. That one didn't even make sense—his people hadn't had tails for thousands of years. Why make a point of calling attention to it? Monkeys had had tails once too. But regardless, the captain had always addressed him with an insult, usually linked to his species. Never his actual name.

The captain shrugged and turned away, his eyes going back to Velma. "Hell of a night, kid. When the civilians go nuts, cops have to stick together. Now go to fucking sleep. We'll need you in the morning."

"Good night, sir." Gaurav slipped out the door, his head spinning. The world was upside-down, and he couldn't tell who the good guys and bad guys were anymore. If only he could talk to Kris, for just five minutes. That would be enough.

Gaurav stood outside the hospital, in the midst of a crowd of angry, anxious people. Some were crying. Others were shouting, enraged, or trying to be. Trying to submerge their fear in a sea of anger. If you were loud enough, you might not feel the terror. It was cold, much too cold, but at least in the middle of the crowd the wind couldn't get to you as much.

The others would be at Amara's parents' house by now. Gaurav had choices—he could go join them. He could try to find Kimmie. He could go home.

His boss had sent him home, and home was tempting. It was just another shitty apartment, but the curving grey walls would be comforting. It would be warm; Gaurav paid extra to keep the heat turned up. And Kris was there—his ashes, at least. Kris had no immediate relatives, and his more distant ones hadn't laid claim. And so they'd come to his partner to deal with. Most cops would have scattered them in the ocean, or the jungle, or one of the city gardens marked for such things. Maybe Gaurav would do that too, someday, but right now he liked having Kris close enough to talk to at night.

He could go there right now, talk it all over with him—but home was ten minutes away. Ten minutes might be critical tonight. Gaurav checked his net connection—1:45. Still hours left, but with no idea what to do, or how much time it might take.

Home, Amara's house, Kimmie. There was another choice. He could leave. Go to the spaceport, hire a ship. The ships were all grounded, but he was sure some were leaving nonetheless. He couldn't afford passage, but he was a cop. He could access the banks and take out as much money as he needed. If Gaurav showed up at the port with his pockets stuffed with hard credits, *someone* would take him on board. He'd be a criminal then, and they'd come after him. But there was a war on. People got lost in a war, and how much manpower could they spare to chase down a thief when mass murder threatened? And once he was out there, in the stars, maybe he could do some good. There would be people on his home planet who would be scared, might even be under threat. He hadn't seen his parent-clutch in so long.

It was a pleasant fantasy, and on another night, Gaurav might have lingered with it. But tonight, there was no time—the plan was born, considered, and died within moments. There was no time for fantasy tonight. Just facts—there was a threat to the peace, official channels had failed, and Gaurav couldn't run away. Wouldn't. If you take an action, you must also accept the consequences of that action; that was another of Kris's sayings. Gaurav couldn't live with the consequences of running away from the people he'd sworn to protect.

There was only one choice, really. Amara might or might not be successful in enlisting her mother's help. Regardless, they'd need Kimmie, or someone like her. The thunder was closer now, and the rain pelted him with icy needles. Wind whipped through the street, fierce enough now to quiet the frenzied crowd, sending them huddling against the walls of the building, pressing in, as best they could, through the hospital doors. He wasn't sure the flyer could take this weather, but right now, it didn't have to. 1:52. Kimmie lived just a few blocks away; he didn't know if she could help, or would. He barely knew the girl; he didn't even know if he would have thought of her, if he hadn't seen her earlier that night. But he had to try.

Letting out a heartfelt groan, Gaurav tensed his muscles, and headed out in a stumbling run.

Dayan out there, in the stars, and she here, stuck in this bed. Cold enough tonight that Uma has pulled the covers up over her body, dressed in its sleep sari. He is flying and she is burrowed deep, a swathe of white linen around her, like a shroud. White for widows, and she isn't a widow, technically, is defiant enough that she wears colors loudly, proudly, during the day. But at night she can't keep it up. At night she surrenders to widow's white and the cold comfort it offers. That he is gone, and there is no need to pretend otherwise, no use in it. He is gone, her husband, her god, her life. Never again to circle the sacred fire with her, wrists bound together by silk, pledging a renewal of love and marriage. Never again to gently criticize her cooking, flirt with her friends, fall asleep on the sofa with chores left undone, and she should be grateful for that, but no. She just wants her husband back, flaws and all. Years now and still she is unreconciled. Her sisters tell her she has too stubborn a heart. Yes. Fine. But how cold must a heart be, that it could abandon all hope of love's return? Of lips bending to touch lips, of hands unwrapping her sari, releasing her from its confines. Here, in bed under the sheets, it is too difficult to unwind, but at least she can pull the fabric up, baring her bent legs, slide it up, up to her thighs, her hips. Delicate linen sliding over aging skin. Even if their gods had allowed it, she couldn't afford the genetic treatments to keep that skin young for a few decades longer. Not that it would be true life extension—no one had managed much of that. But the appearance of youth could be maintained. If Uma had the money, despite her beliefs, the anti-aging therapies would be hard to resist; she is vain enough to dye her hair, after all. At sixty-three, it still falls in a tangled black cloud to her waist, black as a starless night. In the morning, she will brush and braid it; again, that pride. That no one can see the holes in her heart. That pride will destroy her in the end. Because when grief rises up in a sucking midnight tide, a wave that crashes over her and drags her under, she does not call for help. Not her sisters, not her daughters, not the temple congregants. She does not call her few remaining friends, the ones who ignore how sharp her tongue has become since Dayan flew up and away. Uma battles it out alone in the night, her thighs wet and open, one hand buried between them and the other balled up against her mouth. Holding back the sounds, the cries of pleasure mixed with bitter pain. Every night she dies for lack of him, her husband, her god. Lost to the empty sky and lost to her. While she lies bound tight as an antique mummy in their desolate marriage bed.

Part III: The City Divided

Omnis Civitas Contra Se Divisa:
All the city divided against itself
will not remain.

Slowly We Gather

"But why did you think I could help you?" Uma frowned at them, and Narita tried to stifle her flinch. After Amara had left her so abruptly, Narita had blamed everyone, but especially Uma.

She'd known that Amara's mother disliked her, or at least disapproved of her. How could she not know that? The woman, scrupulously polite, offered samosas and sambar but never a smile. Uma hadn't known that Narita and Amara were dating—or at least, Narita had thought she hadn't known. Now, she wasn't so sure. She remembered Uma as a colorful, energetic figure. But Narita didn't know this woman standing in front of her, in white sari, tired brown skin, mad tangles of black hair. Her cheekbones jagged, cheeks sunken. Limbs long and thin and sharp; an artist's chiaroscuro representation of war and grief.

Amara said, "Amma, please. You know everyone; you organize every temple event. I think I've figured out some of what we need, but we need people to implement it. Both people with skills and without. If Gaurav's friend can get the gate open, then we can get to the main corridor leading to the computer lab. I'm not sure what will work best, but we thought it would be better to avoid a full-on assault. Chieri suggested sleeping gas, pumped in through the vents. But we'd need sleeping gas, or the components for it, and something to block up the vents, and ideally some gas masks." Amara's voice getting faster, higher-pitched; she was starting to panic. Narita stifled a pang of sympathy. "It's all very complicated, and we only have five hours left. If that. We can't be sure they'll really wait until dawn. They could set off the missiles any minute, so we have to act fast. We may just have to storm in there, without weapons even, and hope that a huge crowd of bodies will be enough to stop them."

Uma said, her voice trembling, "But why do you want me to

do it? Why ask me, ask our friends to risk their lives? Who are these people you're spending time with, kunju? I don't like it. Devadesis and policemen. And this one." That was directed to Narita, although Uma still wouldn't look her in the eye. "These are not our sort of people. You know mixing only leads to trouble. Look at your uncle, married a white girl, and see what it's gotten him?"

"Amma!" Amara was blushing, Narita knew, was hideously embarrassed, but there was nothing Narita could do to make this easier for her. She wasn't sure she wanted to anyway. If Amara had been braver, a decade ago, Narita's relationship with Uma might be very different now.

Uma said, tiredly, "Go home to your husband, kunju. He must be so worried about you, out on terrible night like this. You have a husband, you should be grateful."

Amara hesitated a moment, and then said, her voice drained of expression, "He cheated on me."

Narita hadn't known that, had avoided asking Amara anything personal since she'd arrived on her doorstep. But she wasn't surprised. When she'd heard that Amara had married, Narita had followed—no, stalked—Amara's husband, Rajiv. For months, actually, trying to figure out what he had that she hadn't; Narita had followed him from class to class, and all she'd discovered was that he was popular with his students, male and female, human and alien. Rajiv was a charismatic, entertaining lecturer, and he gave easy A's. That was apparently enough to justify a certain amount of rather obvious lechery—none of the students seemed to mind his off-color jokes and lewd Shakespearean references. Apparently it had gone further.

Uma shrugged. "So?"

Amara's eyes sparked then, and her voice sharpened. "So I left him."

"Foolish girl." Uma's own voice empty, dispassionate. Like it was echoing from the depths of a very black hole.

Amara stepped forward, took her mother's limp hand in both of her own hands. "Amma, please."

Uma sighed. "You will give me no peace, I can see that. Perhaps we will all die tomorrow. I will send your message out."

Amara hugged her then, quick and hard. "Priority, Amma. Wake them up, please."

The small woman shrugged again. "Why not? What does it matter if any of them talk to me ever again?"

Narita looked around the room, bewildered. Was this was what Amara had had in mind? Uma must have a tremendous amount of clout, because when she'd sent a priority message at 1:30 in the morning to over a hundred people, they'd all shown up on her doorstep within half an hour. Okay, not quite all—a few had put pillows over their echoing heads, determinedly ignoring the ringing emergency alert. A handful had ignored the call, but the rest were here, crowded into the small house, spilling out, despite the increasingly bad weather, into the tiny sunken garden. Young and old—squalling babies on the arm of tired parents, grandfathers and great-grandfathers leaning on canes, a cross-section of unmodified humanity, brown-skinned, colorfully dressed, and loud.

Narita didn't think there were more than half-a-dozen people who had ever given her priority override access to their net connections; it was an in-case-of-emergencies, like your emergency contact at the doctor, and she'd never known anyone to actually use the option. But this woman—she had priority access to her whole temple congregation. Maybe it wasn't so surprising after all, that Uma's huband had taken himself off to the sky to commune with their gods; clearly, in her own very different way, Uma was equally committed to their religion, or at least to its community.

Everyone was so warm to Amara, and by extension, to Narita. *Call me aunty, call me uncle,* was the refrain of the hour. They kept touching Narita—pats on the shoulder, two-handed handshakes, kisses on both cheeks, and more than a few hard embraces. She could remember the last time she had been touched by so many people in such a short space of time. They treated her like family—and as Amara had explained in a hasty whisper, they actually *were* her family. The community intermarried often, and as a result, almost everyone here was related to Amara by blood or marriage.

In Narita's own family, that would have meant they all looked alike; humods tended to choose to emphasize family resemblances in their children. Similar hair color, eye color, face and body shapes. All the women in her own family were tall and slender, small-breasted and small-hipped. Amara used to tease her, that Narita didn't have enough curves to wear a sari properly—*you need breasts and bottom to look good in a sari!* She'd been teasing, but it had still stung a bit, and maybe she had meant it to, since Amara spent a lot of time fretting about her own shape. Narita hadn't chosen to look the way she did, but now, looking around this sea of misshapen bodies, every man and woman shorter than she was, Narita couldn't help but be grateful for her parents' choices.

In her medical training, even though she was specializing in aliens, Narita had seen plenty of unmodified humans. But it was different, being crowded in with them, with the flesh and blood and stink of them. God, they stank; it was hard to breathe, even with the filters going full blast. At least the stench of unmodified human flesh was being covered up, somewhat, by the rising scents of onion, ginger, and garlic, mustard and cumin seed, all tempered in rich ghee.

Amazingly, in the midst of this crisis, they were cooking.

Despite the cacophony of voices and the crowding, it was oddly peaceful in Uma's house. Perhaps it was the lack of screens. At her parents' penthouse, the west screen wall would be on right now, full display showing a dozen different news channels, playing the video of the missile atack over and over. Her mother would be awake, even at this hour, online with her friends, voyeuristically rehashing the details. Not frightened, of course—they would all be sure nothing like this could ever happen to *them*. More excited; it was all so thrilling, wasn't it?

Narita could find a screen somewhere in here, watch the video herself, but it felt wrong. She'd called into the university hospital earlier, not long after Jequith arrived at her apartment, just to see if they could use her. But they had plenty of fully-trained doctors working on the non-human patients that had come in; they quote "didn't want a trainee cluttering the place up" unquote. It must be chaos there. Narita had spent time in the Warren, training at the smaller clinic there. An invaluable opportunity to get some field experience treating non-humans, and in her months there, she had assisted in treating all sorts. Her favorites might be the Rymisians, who never seemed to travel in packs smaller than thirty or so, which would have been overwhelming, if they weren't the size of human three-year-olds. Actually, they were still overwhelming, but they were also so damn cute, it didn't matter. She supposed it was a survival mechanism—their soft fur, chirping voices, big eyes. Not a survival mechanism that would have helped them against a rocket attack.

There were several packs of Rymisians living in the Warren, clustered in a few large apartment buildings; one of their buildings might easily have been hit. If a patient of hers had died tonight, Narita didn't want to know. Didn't want to watch their suffering on a screen. The people of the Warren had lost so much, at least she could offer them a little privacy. Futile, but what else could she do? Except, of course, what she *was* doing—coming together with these people to try to prevent another, perhaps worse, tragedy from happening.

She knew, if needed, Amara would call on her for funds. Looking around, it was clear that no one here had the resources she had—you could see it in their dress, their speech, their skin. But it didn't seem like throwing credits at the problem would solve much tonight. Narita felt oddly helpless. Left to herself, she might have gone back to bed, pulled the covers over her head, and waited for morning. Instead she was being towed along in Amara's wake.

Narita escaped to the garden, allowing the press of bodies to carry her outside. It was still loud out here, voices raised in argument, but not as overhwelmingly so as indoors. As the weather worsened,

most people were trying to crowd back inside. The rain had turned
to hard little ice pellets—hail, she thought it was called, though
she had never seen or felt it before. It was freezing, and Narita
shivered, staring up at the stars. What was happening up there?
Were there starships exchanging torpedoes even now? She checked
the net—nothing out in space, not yet. The news commentators
were still talking about the buildings that had collapsed—they
were up to seven dead now, from a single rocket. Bad, but it could
be so much worse.

This plan of Amara's—it could kill them all. But if she died
tonight, at least Narita would die standing on a planet's surface,
would fall to the ground. It would be better, she thought, than
dying in the cold emptiness of space. Narita actually had no idea
what weapons starships carried, or how a space battle might be
carried out. There were plenty of versions in books and holos,
complete with impossible sound effects and beautiful explosions.
But in all her life, she'd never heard of an actual space battle. Kriti's
planetary defense systems had never been used, in the hundreds
of years since colonization. The skies were usually so peaceful.
How had they come to this?

"You look cold, dear." An old man draped a shawl around her
shoulders as she looked down, startled. He'd actually had to stand
on a nearby garden chair in order to reach, but he seemed quite
steady there, his chappals abandoned on the ground, and his toes
curled around the wrought iron seat.

"Thank you—but you must be freezing." Narita gestured to
his bare shoulders and feet; he was dressed only in a thin batik
sarong. He must have given her the shawl off his own back. She
started to remove it, but he waved her away.

"Oh, I only wear that to please my wife. I don't feel the cold
anymore. There's not much left of me now—not enough to
shiver." He smiled, and indeed, he seemed barely there, flesh and
bone and a scrap of fabric.

She hesitated, hands twisted in the warm wool fabric. "Still, I
should give this back to you before I go."

"Are you going somewhere, dear?"

"Yes. No. I'm not sure what I'm doing here," Narita softly confessed. At Chieri's house, Amara had taken charge, had formulated a vision, a plan, and dragged them all along. Even now, Chieri was rounding up her devadasi friends, preparing a second attack option, while Gaurav searched for his computer expert. And what could Narita offer? Nothing, unless people got hurt.

And yes, that was her job, to heal, and she should go with them. People were bound to get hurt in this mad endeavour. But there were hurt people at the hospital too—she could go there now and help. If she went to the hospital, Narita would be ready when these people failed, when the missiles went off, when the Warren was obliterated. Ready to help those who survived the blast. Narita would be safe at the hospital, and might even be of more use. At the hospital, she wouldn't have to endure Uma's glares, or the continuous stares and muttered comments from Amara's relatives and community. There were a hundred reasons why she should go, but none of them seemed enough.

He looked down at her, and raised an eyebrow. "You're here because you love her."

"What?" Narita said, startled.

"It's in your eyes. I, Karthik, say so, and I see better than most!" He grinned. "Though the truth is, anyone can see it, child; you're practically shouting your love to the skies every time you look at her."

"I can't love her," Narita protested. She wouldn't love Amara, wouldn't allow it. She had spent a decade erecting walls to protect her heart from Amara, from love itself—that was what Chieri always claimed. Chieri didn't approve; she said such rejection of love was a denial of the gods, was sacrilege. But Chieri wasn't here. What was Narita doing, talking of love to this stranger, in the midst of a storm of frozen hail? And yet, what else should she be doing, right now? The world turned upside down.

"Ah, you mean it's not safe to love her." He offered a twisted smile. "If there's one lesson of this night, dearest, it's that nothing is safe."

Narita asked, "Aren't you scared?" The words just tumbled out, and she immediately felt bad for asking. But Karthik was so calm and cheerful, a tiny gnarled gnome of a man. He didn't seem real.

He shrugged. "To tell the truth, I'm terrified. You would think someone as old as I would be reconciled to death, would be ready for it. But, child, the closer death comes, the more I love life. I want to grab every moment I can; I want each one to last a lifetime." Karthik frowned, and continued, "But it must be right sort of life, no? We must choose the path of dharma, of virtue and righteousness. That is what our pandit taught us, before he left us. That is what Uma teaches us still, for all the bitter edge to her now."

"But what if you don't know what the virtuous path is?"

He smiled. "Well, that's what I was saying before. Follow your heart, follow your love. Seventy years married, and that's one lesson I'm sure of. If you are true to the one you love, if you strive to be the person they deserve—then you will find the right path. It might not be an easy path, but it will be the right one." Karthik grinned then. "That's not exactly what the pandit preached, or his wife. But it works for me."

Narita bit her lip, considering. But before she could speak, a raised male voice echoed from inside. "Why should we help them? They're all just as bad, the humods with their noses up in the air, the aliens who look at us like we're insects. Insects they'd like to eat." The voice was rising, almost into a shriek. "Maybe we'd be better off, if they were blasted off the face of the planet."

Narita felt her skin grow even colder, despite the shelter of the shawl. Should she say something? Whomever was speaking, he must have seen her standing here. She towered over them all, like a giant. Like a target. But before she could say anything, even if she'd had the nerve, a sharp voice responded loudly, "Suthil, you're a fool. You've always been a fool, and age hasn't brought you any wisdom. Go home, man. Go home!" And the murmurs of the crowd seemed to support that command. Narita took a deep breath, forcing herself to relax.

The old man shook his head, and then hopped down from the chair. "Child, you mustn't worry about the maunderings of fools like Suthil. In times like these, there will always be those who let fear rule them. But you're among family here; no one will harm you." He patted her on the arm, gently. "Now we must go back inside; we don't want to miss the decision. They've been arguing long enough; you can hear it if you listen. They're coming to a decision. I think I know which way Uma and the rest will jump, but you never know—they might surprise me still. Regardless, though—my wife and I are with you, child."

Before Narita could protest, or give back his shawl, Karthik was gone, disappearing into the crowd. Leaving her trembling again, though this time, not from the cold.

"Vani Aunty, please!" In the kitchen, Amara was fighting a losing battle with the loudest of her great-aunts, a scrawny old woman hefting another enormous platter of samosas to the table. It looked like it weighed more than she did. "We don't have time!"

Vani frowned. "Kunju, you've woken us up in the middle of the night. No one can think if they're hungry. Even soldiers have the sense to eat before they go into battle. Have some chai, have a samosa. You'll feel better."

Narita had to silently agree, her mouth full of samosa. Apparently, Uma kept a freezer stocked with samosas for the reception after the temple services—a quick fry and they were ready to go. Gods, she'd forgotten what good cooks Amara's family were, even though they were completely vegan. When you could cook like this, you didn't miss milk and cheese. The green chili chutney was searingly hot, the tamarind chutney was dark and sweet, and mixed together and poured over a spicy samosa, they were heaven on earth.

A minute ago, suffocating in the crowd, deafened by the noise of people arguing, shouting, Narita had been fighting the urge to burst into tears. It was bad enough that she'd lost control at Chieri's house—it wouldn't be the first time the devadasi had seen her cry.

But she couldn't do it here, not in front of Amara's mother. It would be too humiliating. Thank the gods the samosas and tea had come to her rescue. Strong and sweet; after tea, Narita felt as if she could face anything. Even a mob of madmen with missiles. And now they had their own mob.

Amara obstinately refused the offered plate; she stood there, arms crossed and determined. How often had Narita seen her like this, back when they were together? It had been irritating then, but endearing, too. The intensity of her, the stubborn passion. Against her will, Narita could feel the walls around her heart starting to crumble. Amara was barely a foot away, across the table. She'd pulled her hair back, into a messy bun, when they'd set out from Chieri's house; it was starting to unravel now, in the hot, humid press of the kitchen crowd. Narita fought the urge to reach out, brush an errant curl away from that tired face. She shouldn't. She'd been down this road before.

Vani clapped her hands, and the crowd in the kitchen fell silent, though the murmur from the further rooms and garden continued unabated. Uma had faded to the background; she leaned against a wall, clearly exhausted. Apparently she'd played her part in bringing them all here; Vani appeared to be in charge now. "We have a plan, dearest," Vani explained. "It's almost 2:30 now, yes?"

"Yes!" Amara's assent was firm, impatient.

"We think Raju Uncle can get sleeping gas from the factory. He looked up the recipe online; it's not so hard. In fact, it's a little disturbing, how easy it is to make—but we can worry about that later."

Amara's face brightened. "That's great, Aunty!"

Vani lifted a hand in caution. "It will take him some time, though. That's all right, though—we'll need that time to get the pump."

"Where are you going to get the pump from?"

Vani bit her lip. "I am afraid you will have to steal it."

"What?" Amara said, her eyes widening.

"Your friend has access to the hospital, yes?"

Narita swallowed, as all eyes turned to her. "I—I have limited access to some restricted areas. They let the students observe…"

Vani nodded firmly. "That will help. There is machinery there that we can use. Karthik thinks he can adapt it to our needs. The four of us will go, together—too many, and we'll be noticed."

Amara protested, "But we still haven't figured out how to get the gate open."

Vani said calmly, "Yes, that is a problem. The rest of the group will stay here and work on it; with this many people thinking hard, they may come up with a solution. Or perhaps your policeman friend will find help. A path will be opened for us, I am sure."

"Aunty, you can't be sure. Not really." Amara's truculence had fallen away, leaving a strange vulnerability behind. Had Narita ever seen her like this? Frightened and lost, seeking comfort? Oh, yes. The walls crumbled further. Earlier this evening, when Amara had knocked on her door—when Narita had opened it, Amara had looked exactly like this. Narita just couldn't see it then.

Uma stepped forward then, away from the wall. The crowd parted for her, like water around a stone. "Kunju, quiet yourself. You are doubting yourself, and I know I was harsh with you when you came. But I have been listening to our people for the past half hour, listening and thinking and I tell you, you were right. Right to come here, right to have me wake all of these people, right to ask us to fight with you."

"This isn't your problem," Amara said softly. "You don't like aliens. You think genetic modification is against the will of the gods."

Uma frowned. "Aliens are so different, that it is easy for us to misstep with them, or they with us. It is safer to keep to our own kind. And I find genemod…troubling. We have been given these bodies for a purpose, and to blithely reshape them, often for no reason beyond vanity—that seems the height of arrogance."

Narita winced, and wished she could make herself smaller. Not that she had chosen her mods, but still…

Uma went on, her gaze focused on her daughter. "But that

doesn't mean I think the humods are evil, child. They are just people. I may not think genetic modification is right for me—but it is not my place to decide that for anyone else. In the end, each of us must find our own path to the gods, no matter what others think. Your father was clear on that, at least." Her voice shook for a moment, and then steadied. "And searching for the right path does not absolve us from our duty to each other. Those aliens who live in the Warren—they may not be human. But if the gods want anything from us, they want us to take care of each other, no matter how strange we may seem to one another."

The room was silent now, all the murmurs fallen away, as if the pandit's wife were offering a temple lesson. Narita supposed she was. Uma reached out now and ran a gentle hand through Amara's unkempt hair, soothing it down. Narita could almost see Amara calming at her mother's touch. Uma smiled—a bleak smile, true, but it was still a smile, and in that moment, beautiful. "We've always taken care of each other in this community, haven't we? Haven't I always taught you that?"

"Yes, amma," her daughter said, looking chastened.

"I do not know if we will have the strength to stop these evil men. But that does not absolve us from the responsibility to try. And now, we must pray."

Amara protested, "*Now*, amma?"

Uma took her daughter's hand in hers. "Especially now. We needed food, to make our bodies strong for the fight ahead. And we need prayer, to make our hearts strong. It will not take long. Come, kneel with me." They knelt together on the slatted wood floor, the rest of the crowd following to their knees in a swift rustling.

Narita sat at the table, awkwardly, until Uma reached out to her with her other hand. "You too, child. You are one of us now, are you not?"

A great yearning opened up in her heart, and without warning, the walls came crashing down. Oh yes, yes.

Narita was so tired, so scared. And it was too hard to keep her defenses up now—not when all her energy was needed for this new fight. What Amara had done, all those years ago, didn't matter. Not now, in this moment. And it didn't matter how flawed these people were, how smelly and ugly and imperfect. They were still beautiful.

This was a terrible night, the beginning, perhaps, of many terrible nights. Narita slid to her knees beside Uma, taking her hand. She didn't know much right now—she certainly didn't know if she and Amara could be together again—but she knew one thing at least.

She didn't want to fight this battle alone. If these people, this family, wanted her, she was theirs.

Sparks Fly

Kimsriyalani slipped down through the layers of code. She didn't usually go deep—it wasn't her way. She preferred the bright, flashing surface, laying intricate patterns that coruscated in the light, like sunlight on the waves. Oh, she knew, of course, that darker patterns lurked below—that was part of the fun of it, dancing on the surface of the water, knowing that a single misstep would send you crashing down to the depths.

She never crashed, of course. Not her, and not her programs, not since she was a youngling learning to navigate the code-net. They'd started her simply, with manual inputs, but when those grew too slow, her school had sponsored the cost of an implant. Implants were rare on Varisia—most of her people preferred the life of the body strongly enough that they eschewed even the simple net connections that were standard here on Pyroxina for all but the very poorest.

Kimsriyalani loved the pulsebeat of life as much as any of her people, the rush of blood under the skin, the pounding of feet and heart in chase through the hanging vines and quicksand pits of the Jungle. But her heart was divided; with the implant she'd found a new love in the net. The net-world might be thin, attenuated, compared to meat-space. But here, finally, connections sprang into being as fast as she could imagine them; her code spiraled up in delicate minarets and cascading towers. Sometimes she would fall into coding so hard and fast that only the fierce rumble of her stomach could drag her out again, hours later.

She'd been eating when the campus guard arrived, shoveling vat-steak into her mouth with fierce concentration. Kimsriyalani had come from her midnight park encounter cleansed and invigorated. She had showered, and then fallen into coding. With the scent of the human still lingering despite her best efforts—not that he had smelled unpleasant, but she preferred to be clean—she had fallen back into her dissertation. Kimsriyalani was close to finishing— had been close for months, it seemed. But she'd gotten stuck on one particularly tricky patch of code that refused to behave. Stuck until tonight, because now, she could see a way through. It would be convoluted, complex, but she could see it clear. Maybe the human's cock had cleared the way—the thought amused her. If this actually worked, she would hunt him down. Learn his name, maybe even dedicate her dissertation to him.

She'd blazed through the work, piece after piece falling into place, until finally she had to stop and eat something. But she could see it now, the way through, and if the goddess smiled, Kimsriyalani would reach the end by dawn. Just a few more bites of bloody fake meat, a few more hours of work, and she could hand this damn thing in, graduate, and be off this planet for good. Head out into the stars; a thousand companies would want to hire her when this was done, especially if she brought the patent for the weaponry with her. Especially with a war on, because it was weapons she was designing, oh yes.

Her first dissertation had been purely defensive, but she had been so enraged after what he'd done to her, Kimsriyalani had turned her claws outward. Anyone who attacked one of her systems wouldn't simply be repulsed—no, her program would track him down, sniff out his hiding places, drag him out and excavate him, flesh and blood and bone. Fine, it wouldn't be quite that bloody, or that quickly implemented. But it would be final, when the program was finished. Just a few more hours…and then, the buzzer snarled at her. Just past two in the morning and someone at the door. Had the human followed her home? She hadn't intended a second bout tonight, but if he were offering, she might take him up on it. She deserved to celebrate. It was a fine plan, but it came crashing down when she eagerly pulled open the door, only to see a lizard face.

She hissed, reflexively. He mantled in response. Then both of them took a step back, mutually embarrassed by their inherited instincts. He said, "Kimmie?"

"Kimsriyalani," she replied, firmly. She was going to have to do a lot of correcting for a while. For as long as she was stuck here. "I know you." The policeman, Kris's partner.

"Gaurav. I was Kris's partner."

"You're the only saurian on this gods-forsaken planet; you're hard to forget."

His wrinkly face frowned. "Of course. Sorry—it's been a strange night. There's something I need to talk to you about. Can I come in?"

Kimsriyalani tensed. Had it been illegal, fucking the human in the park? Probably, but it seemed strange that anyone would care about that on a night like this. As they'd finished, the news had come over their connections, marked urgent—a missile had exploded in the Warren. Later, she'd learned that people had died, though thankfully, no one she knew. Surely this Gaurav had better things to do with his time? But still—she was almost done, almost out of here. The last thing she needed was trouble with the police. Kimsriyalani took a step back, and gestured him inside. The hallway was narrow, and he brushed her fur as he past. She fought back the urge to bristle.

Gaurav refused her offer of steak, but accepted tea. She had learned to like it the way the humans drank it here—strong, with milk and jaggery. Over their cups, he explained what had happened tonight. The whore, the drugged human, the threat, the plan. He asked if she could, if she would, help. By the time he finished, it was almost three, and her eyes were wide with shock. Kimsriyalani could so easily be living in the Warren too—the only reason she wasn't was the human man who'd betrayed her. This was his apartment; after he'd stolen her research and published it as his own, she'd kicked him out and taken it over.

She said quietly, "What you want from me—it's illegal."

"Yes," Gaurav admitted.

"If I were caught, I would be kicked out of my program."

"Probably."

She fought the urge to extrude her claws; if she weren't careful, she could crush the fragile china teacup. A little destruction might relieve her tension, but she would regret the loss later. "Nobody would hire me. I'd have to go back to Varisia as an utter failure."

"I'm sorry." He seemed sincere.

"And I don't even know if I can do what you want." Kimsriyalani had specialized in building defenses, and building weapons. Would those help her with opening a Gate? She had no idea.

Gaurav said only, "If you could try, we would appreciate it."

She pressed him. "But *we* is just a bunch of people. Not the official police, or the university, or the city."

"That's right." His tone was so calm, despite the minutes ticking away as she considered. As if Gaurav didn't want to push her one way or another, which was funny, considering how desperate he must be, to come to her like this, in the middle of the night.

There were a hundred reasons not to do it. But in her arteries and veins, her blood was rising, pumping harder, faster. Her calf muscles clenched, claws digging into the wood floor, scraping deep gouges. Kimsriyalani carefully put the tea cup down on the table, and then—she couldn't help herself. She threw her head back and laughed. This was ridiculous; it was insane. To risk the last decade of work, her entire future? But she couldn't say no. If she had endured the trials of the Jungle to prove that she retained some of the virtues of her people's barbaric past, perhaps now it was time to prove herself civilized as well. These people, this planet, might be going down in flames, but she could at least try to help them.

"All right, then. Let's get to work."

And it was easy, after all, to slide down the levels, from the familiar surface to the fathomless deeps. She could feel it tearing at her mind, the scattered flashes of neurons as she raced defensive code from top to bottom; she would take some damage from this, no doubt. But there was Kali's Gate, rising up before her in all its majesty. There was the lock—and oh, she could tease it open, given enough time. Time she didn't have, to study the problem, to learn the paths to its heart. But there were other ways to open a Gate, and one of them, she carried with her. Her code; her beautiful al-most-completed code. Completed enough for this, to melt the code that held the Gate locked, the final barrier to the computer lab. Those inside wouldn't even know their lock had failed, not until Gaurav's people burst through—not unless they tried to open it themselves, of course. Which could happen, but she couldn't control everything. She could do this, though.

It would hurt, doing it this way, the flash bright enough to burn out some neurons. But she would likely survive. And there was no time to do it the slow way, no time, and truth be told, no desire. Tonight, she was aching for a fight. Kimsriyalani braced herself in front of the gates, stretched out a long, muscled arm, and lay one clawed finger on the gate. She said, softly, a single word. "Boom."

And the world exploded.

And Brightly Blaze

Vani tried not to trip over her sari as they hurried through the hospital corridors; she had dressed hastily, in the dark, and had skipped her usual pins to secure the folds, which were now water-soaked and dragging on the floor. Tripping would be embarrassing, especially in front of the children. Not that they thought of themselves as children, she was sure, but from the perspective of almost-ninety, Narita and Amara were as new-hatched chicks, fluttering around each other in an agony of hunger and confusion. Karthik stumbled behind her, and she tried not to fret for him. Her husband was a decade older than she was; too old for this madness. He'd managed to pawn off his shawl on Narita at some point at Uma's house; Karthik hated wearing it, and always shed it at the first opportunity, no matter how she nagged.

With his heart problems, he should really be at home, tucked up in bed. The bed where they had been so sweetly occupied before Uma's call shattered their peace. Well, not peace exactly. Not anything like peace at all, to be honest, more of a raging frenzy. And how *that* would shock the children, if they knew, if they could have seen Vani and her husband, stark naked under the brightly-embroidered bedspread, sweaty wrinkled limbs frantically entwined.

Vani had done the embroidery work for their fiftieth anniversary, had chosen figures from the Kama Sutra to execute in shimmering silver and gold. Vani wasn't the sort to give tours of her home, and as a result, she felt free to express herself as she desired, especially in her bedroom. She desired a lot. Bodies cavorted across the covers in silken thread, and across the floor in glittered mosaic, and over the walls in faded paint. She and Karthik would never lack for inspiration in that room.

She really ought to refresh those murals, although Vani was

getting old enough to be a bit unsteady on a ladder. No matter—
Karthik could hold it for her. Perhaps she would wear a short-
skirted dress for him, and skip the underwear. After seventy years
of marriage, she could still give her husband a thrill, and maybe
that was why they were still married, after seventy years. Every five
years, regular as the monsoon rains, they would walk out to the
garden where they'd first wed and renew their vows, signing the
document that said yes, yes, I will marry you again. Five-year contracts might be traditional, but sometimes Vani wished they'd chosen one-year contracts instead. Just for the joy of signing them,
again and again and again.

Oh, her mind was rambling tonight. It should be on what they
were doing, but really, she had little to contribute here, aside from
the drive to get it done, the focus on what was important. That
had always been her gift; it was how they'd found the time to
work, both of them, despite temple and children and house and
garden, despite all the demands of the world. She had kept them
focused—Karthik at his wood and metalwork, she at her textiles.
The two of them now solid in their careers, their reputation, their
art. Although there was always more to achieve. Art was the true
mistress, with a deep and bottomless hunger; she would swallow
you down and demand more and more, every drop of juice in
you, if you let her. She would suck you dry.

Even now Vani wanted to be home, wanted to be drawing or
sewing, her fingers in motion. They hovered at the door, Narita
pressed her hand to the lockplate, they stumbled inside in a great
confusion. Karthik bounded over to the machine they needed,
falling to his knees, pulling tools out of his satchel. The storm
raged outside the windows, lightning flashing; they had all gotten
drenched in the mad rush to the hospital and now they stood,
dripping and cold, under the slowly whirring fans. The children
would not look at each other; they stood as far apart as they reasonably could in this tiny room of mechanical objects. But their
bodies yearned for each other; she could see it in the lines of
tensed muscle, the lift and reach of shoulderblades.

Vani could draw them like this—oh, she was craving her charcoals now. If she had to be here—and where else would she be, when Karthik was in the thick of it—if she had to be here, if only she could have pencil in hand, at least. There was no paper in this room, no writing implements. The most she could do was trigger her net connection to let her draw with her fingers in the air and record it for later use. Bah. That was never as good, never as satisfying as being there, in the moment, with fingers flying and the body burning up with desire.

"Vani, I need you."

She was at his side in an instant, sliding down to her knees, muffled in layers of wet cotton, her pulse racing. "Yes?"

"Here, hold this." One hand pressing two plates of metal together, the other pinching closed a rubber valve. After just a few minutes, her fingers were aching, and her knees, but she wouldn't call one of the children over, not yet. Karthik had asked her, trusted her with this, to partner with him as she had on so many of their projects over the years. In the ordinary way, they'd have years left, but now—nothing was certain now. And she would not give up more than she had to, not a minute, not a moment more than she had to.

Vani could smell the candied fenugreek on his breath, still, that he'd chewed for her not an hour past. She could, kneeling there, trace with her eyes the contours of that bald head, that beak of a nose and out-sticking ears. When she was as young as these children, had she dreamed of beauty? She must have. But what beauty could compare to how dear he was now, each flaw in face and figure more precious to her than gold? They didn't know; they couldn't know. And all she could do was fight for them now, for them all. For herself and Karthik, for the years to come, the years they deserved. And for the children, that they might learn better than they knew now. If they would stop being so stupid, they could be happy.

"Ow!" Karthik swore, and dropped the bolt he held; Vani's heart jumped in her chest.

"What is it?" Amara demanded.

"No, it's nothing. Just a spark." He was already working again, and now she could let go, he was finished, he was holding a metal contraption out to the girls. "That should do it," Karthik said. But he whispered the words, and he was sinking back now, resting against the cold metal. His lips gone grey, and one hand fisted, pressing hard against his chest.

"Uncle—" Amara started to say. But Vani interrupted.

"Run!" she commanded. Vani slid down to rest beside him, back pressed against the bulk of a machine, hands reaching out to pull her husband to her. She was already fumbling in his bag, one hand searching for the medicine he always carried. Karthik knew better than to leave the house without it. She would forgive him the loss of a shawl, but never that. Damnit. Where was it?

Narita was on her knees already, reaching out, "Let me examine him. Is it his heart? This is a hospital; I can find medicine…"

Vani waved her off. "Ah, there! I have his medicine—" she pulled it out, triumphantly, hiding the fear that hammered at her own chest. It might not work. It might be too late. "I will take care of him. You have a larger battle to fight, and we can't help you now. Run, girls! Run!"

They were good girls; they hesitated for a moment longer, and then were gone, obeying her command. Then Vani was popping the pills into her hand, pushing them into his open mouth. Swallow, swallow, my love. Breathe for me. Vani watched him as the storm crashed outside, thunder raging now, and lightning ripping through the sky, one flash after another lighting up his darling face. She timed her breaths with the lightning, with the thunder, with his tortured breaths.

Breathe.

Breathe.

Breathe.

Pric'la had come out despite the storm, despite the thunder and the lightning, no, tell the truth, the truth now, tonight, if no other night. He came out because of the storm, despite every warning and prohibition. His kind could not survive this weather—this whipping wind and slashing rain. His wings furled at his back, fragile rainbow coruscations hidden in silken ribbons of membrane. His wife had not wanted him to go off-planet, had only agreed on condition that he go to Pyroxina Major, which the locals called Kriti, the university planet, where the weather would be climate-controlled throughout the semester. Pric'la had beaten back the rush of excitement at her final acquiescence, had simulated calm as he kissed her and the children goodbye. He ached for them now, their gentle antennae-brushings, their wing-flutters. Pre-speech when he'd left, but by now, now they would be singing, his darlings. And Pric'la was supposed to go back, was supposed to be there in just a few more sun-turnings. He had clung to that through the long days of the semester, his duty to go back keeping him grounded, keeping him at his work. But now, the ships were grounded, now he was trapped on this planet, and thereby released from his duties, his obligations. He could not return in time to see his children launch themselves from the limbs of the world-tree for their first flights. He would not hear their mating cries, or let his mate spin webbing over his face in a final suffocation, giving his body over to feed their new-hatched grubs. Such a death was a father's duty, to enrich the grubs with the nutrients of his body, and Pric'la had resigned himself to it—after all, his life had been long and rich, at least as counted by his own people. But now Pric'la was free, free to be selfish, to find his own ending. His research was done, his books written, and there was nothing left to do but please himself. So up and up he went, climbing the winding stairs of the central tower. Up to the observation platform that he'd dared not visit before. Because he'd known, he'd known, that if he went up there, so high, to stand balanced, precarious, on the spindle that overlooked the vast grounds of the university far below—he'd known that he would not be able to withstand his desires. And oh, the wind beating at him, tearing through him like knives. His thorax swelled and filled with air, with song. Pric'la climbed the tower stairs with trembling, sticky limbs, until finally he clung to the very peak, the apex of the city. Below him, a few lone people scurried through mostly-deserted streets, but he spared only a glance for them before looking to his heart's desire. And there, oh there, crackling through the sky. The storm, the storm, it called to him and he sang his song, his falling, dying song. Pric'la unfurled his wings, and even as he opened them, they tore, as he'd known they must, in this chaos of sound and fury. They tore, and he leapt, and his song ripped through him in a final ecstasy. Shuddering with pain and glory, he flew, and then he fell.

Part IV: A Single Book

Times hominem unius libri:
I fear of a man with a single book.

Phoenix Rises

Rajiv had been startled to get Amara's call. No, more than startled—shocked. Amara had always been so stubborn—when she had walked out of their home, hours before, he had known it was over, the end. And even when she had summoned him to meet her in the middle of the night, he hadn't expected reconciliation. That would have been too unlike her. That would have meant that he didn't know her at all.

He'd been awake. Who could sleep on a night like this? Who could sleep when your wife of a decade had left you, even if you didn't really love her anymore, even if you possibly never had? Rajiv wasn't sure of his own long-ago feelings, though he was sure, now, that Amara had never loved him. He had known that from the beginning, though he had willed himself to ignore it. She was young and pretty enough, and he was grateful that his mother had found him a suitable wife.

It had been difficult to make the transition to tenure-track— being single would have made it even harder. Faculty from the University of All Worlds could take their pick of jobs elsewhere in the galaxy, and other universities dangled golden lures in front of them. It was an open secret that the English department preferred its faculty to be partnered; preferably multiply-partnered with children, for even greater stability, but they would settle for the more common pairings. So, when he was ready to apply for that tenure-track position, Rajiv had told his mother that he was ready for a wife. He had been delighted when she presented Amara. And he really had meant to be faithful.

He should have known better. Maybe if Rajiv had joined a line-marriage or a clan-marriage, he would have done a better job of it.

And now he was standing here, facing the intricate patterns of Kali's Gate in this underground corridor, insulated from the storm overhead. It was eerily quiet here, as the little man with the hand-held pump knelt at a vent, pumping sleeping gas slowly throughout the lower levels. They all wore masks, the whole crowd that Amara had somehow gathered—old men and women along with young, her mother Uma, a cluster of scantily-dressed devadasis, and two aliens—one reptilian, the other feline. A motley crew in their silence and their masks, but even the masks couldn't hide how closely Amara and the woman Narita stood together. Moving in sync. There was something there, and Rajiv was pretty sure he knew exactly what it was. The funny thing was, more than anything, it was a relief.

He had been feeling horribly guilty all night; that was what had dragged him from his comfortable study, through the erupting streets. Someone had thrown a bottle at him, and while it had hit the brick wall instead of his head, the exploding shards had cut his face. Narita had treated the wounds quickly, professionally, when he arrived; only his clothes were bloody now.

Then Amara had gestured at the door lock, and Rajiv had reached out with an only slightly shaking palm.

They'd broken through the deeper security system somehow; Kali's Gate was unlocked, apparently, giving them access to the deepest levels of the building. They hadn't actually opened it yet, just in case opening the Gate would set off an alarm. But the alien, Kimsriyalani, claimed it would open for them now.

Rajiv would have been no use to them with the Gate. But they'd needed to get through the upper doors first, the blast doors that shut off the tunnels to the classrooms in case of emergency. Their computer wizard had said it would take too long to hack through them, but any faculty member could easily open those doors. It had been almost four-thirty in the morning, and so Amara had called him. Her husband. Soon to be ex-husband. And Rajiv had come, stomach churning, head aching and bloodied. He had come for her. He'd opened all the doors.

Narita was speaking softly to Amara. "You're sure you don't want to call Jequith, ask it to come join us? It would be a formidable fighter, and there's no guarantee the gas will work. We may still have to fight."

Amara shook her head wearily. "It just had a baby, and its mate is still injured, healing. I can't bear to ask it to leave its family, not tonight. You understand."

Narita nodded, seeming relieved. They'd barely spoken since he'd arrived, but there was a connection between the two women, thrumming, electric. Rajiv felt a flash of arousal, accompanied by regret. Their lives might have gone so differently, if he had made different choices. Or maybe that was arrogance, to think that. Maybe this was never about him at all.

Narita stepped away to speak to one of the old women, leaving a little space where Rajiv and Amara might talk with a semblance of privacy.

"You can go home now," Amara said to him softly, over the hiss of the pump. She met Rajiv's eyes squarely—she wasn't embarrassed to have left her husband, clearly. But she didn't seem angry either, which surprised him. "Thank you for your help."

"Do you think so little of me?" Rajiv was surprised to find that it hurt.

She hesitated, then said, "I just—I hated to call on you for a favor."

"This isn't for you, or about you," he said quietly. That was mostly true. Rajiv would have come for her, if she'd called, for the decade of marriage, for the vows he'd taken, and broken. But this was bigger than that, bigger than all of them.

She smiled thinly. "You're a professor, not a fighter."

"And these people are fighters?" He gestured to the gathered crowd, a few steps away, but undoubtedly listening to every soft-spoken word between them. Let them listen. "Besides—this is my city, my university. Some of my students live in the Warren." His voice had raised on those words, involuntarily.

Rajiv remembered his father, the physics professor, so angry that his son was going into English instead. Bad enough that English had become the lingua franca of the human race among the stars—worse, that his Tamil son would deliberately choose to embrace it. His father had never, not till the day he died, understood Rajiv's love for the language and its literature. But his father had loved the students too. If Amara's call had come for his father, the old man would have been right beside her, on the barricades, shaking his cane and shouting defiance.

Not that any of them were shouting here. This was the quietest battle Rajiv had ever heard of. Amara was still gazing at him, eyes steady on his. He said softly, "I have a responsibility here. And besides—there might be more doors beyond the gate."

She nodded then, accepting his place among them. Rajiv shivered. The truth was, in the pit of his stomach, he did long to be home, wrapped in an old afghan his mother had crocheted when he was a boy, huddled beside the fire, safe and alone. But there were children to be protected tonight. He'd always hoped to have children someday.

"We're ready," the man by the pump said into the silence. "I've given them everything we have. Either they're asleep or they're not—no way to tell but by going down to see."

Amara took a deep breath, and Rajiv realized that his wife was trembling. She was not so untouched by this night as she had seemed. He reached out then, gripped Amara's shoulder with a reassuring hand. If he could, he would hold her up for this.

Amara reached up and clasped his hand with hers. It felt like an apology and forgiveness, wrapped in one. Just for a moment, and then she released his hand and was gone, moving away into the crowd. They all gathered themselves, silently, as planned. The devadasis in front, ready to charm any who might still be awake inside. Then the strongest amongst them, ready to fight if need be. And the rest, Rajiv among them, a final, desperate rear-guard.

If they lived to see the morning, he would have his mother call the matchmaker again. Amma didn't even know his wife had left him, and he'd have to convince her that it wasn't too soon to start looking for a new wife—or wives. With husbands, even—Rajiv realized, surprised, that he didn't care what kind of marriage he ended up in. He just wanted to be a father. When life was this uncertain, better not to hesitate. He had waited long enough.

Amara gave the signal; Narita stepped forward and pushed the intricate wrought metal. The Gate, silently, swung open.

Dragons Fall

Gaurav had expected it to be harder. They all had. They were amateurs, after all—technically, he was a cop, but he had never trained for, never faced anything like this. But the scene they walked into proclaimed that these would-be conspirators weren't professionals either.

They slumped over computer desks, lolled back on chairs, lay outright on the floor. The gas would have worked quickly, and evidence of that lay all around—spilled chai, scattered flimsies. One man had a bloody nose. They were all asleep. Well, not for long.

Gaurav didn't even need to direct the civilians. They were moving quickly, pulling out lengths of rope from their pockets, tying hands neatly behind the conspirators' backs. He watched, counting. Six. That's all there were—six of them, in casual clothes from the back of beyond. Dhotis and sarongs; old-fashioned button-down shirts. Only one of them dressed more formally, in embroidered salwar kameez. That one had been standing before he fell, in the center of the room. Watching them all, no doubt. That one was the leader.

"Fuck—they had over a hundred of these things rigged up," Kimsriyalani muttered. She was moving quickly from computer to computer, checking them quickly and shutting them down. Gods, it was truly a pleasure to watch her move. It had been so long since Kris—and though he felt faintly guilty for even thinking of another, he also knew that Kris would have laughed and urged him on. It's not as if Kris had been faithful to him, or that Gaurav had even wanted that, particularly. That wasn't their way. It was just that Kris was dead, and a small part of him felt like it would be a betrayal, being with someone alive. Worse—if he touched someone else, kissed someone else, perhaps he would forget what it had been, to be with Kris.

Well. No point speculating tonight—odds were, Kimsriyalani wasn't available, or interested. Most people didn't cross species lines, and just because she'd made an exception for one human earlier tonight, that didn't mean she'd make an exception for Gaurav too. It took a special feline to take a lizard to bed. He wasn't even sure they could do it without their ancestral drives leading them to fight instead. Of course, fighting would be fun too. That was why he'd allowed her insistence on coming along, despite her obvious pain and dizziness after the brilliant hack. She was half a foot taller than anyone else in the room, fiercely muscled; Kimsriyalani would be a magnificent fighter, and Gaurav had feared they'd have need of her.

But apparently not.

"They're shut down now," Kimsriyalani announced, sitting down in an empty chair and spinning to face the crowd. "I don't know where the actual rockets are, but the guidance systems are down; they can't set them off tonight. We're done, with hey, a good half hour to go. The police can take over from here. Which is great, because my head is killing me." She rubbed it ruefully, grinning.

A sigh of relief went through them, and all around the room, people were reaching for chairs, perching on tables. Sixty of them, to the six conspirators, who were now bound securely. It was sufficient; they were safe. So why was Amara still standing in the center of the room, staring down at the well-dressed man, her body thrumming with tension?

"Wake him up," she ordered Narita tersely. "We have to be sure."

Narita looked like she wanted to protest. But she turned to her bag instead, ruffled through a box, pulled out a tab and pressed it to the man's neck. "Two minutes," she said.

They waited. It was almost dawn. Even though Gaurav had now been awake for far more hours than a saurian body was meant to, even though exhaustion dragged at his muscles, so he felt as if he swimming through mud instead of walking, Gaurav's heart was still racing with how close they'd come to failing. Each step had taken time—not much time, but enough to matter. While he raced across the city, talked the captain, flew to Kimsriyalani's, talked her into helping, and watched her take down major security systems, Amara had somehow, bizarrely, found this small horde to help her get a pump, make sleeping gas, find a faculty member, and bring them all here to meet him. At any step along the way, they could have been stymied, sent astray. They could so easily have failed.

And if they had—it had been bad enough at the hospital, seeing the consequences of one rocket. A few deaths, many injured. In the morning, there would be parents grieving their lost and damaged children. In the morning, there would be children crying for parents gone forever. All of that from just one rocket. Gaurav couldn't even imagine the devastation of a hundred landing in the same place. These fools had no idea what they were doing—the force of those missiles would have wreaked havoc and destruction far beyond the Warren; they would have torn a hole in the earth, and ripped the city itself in half. Even here, in this shielded place, the conspirators might not have survived. Hadn't they realized that?

He had been afraid that they'd be confronting trained soldiers here. But these people wore no uniforms. Yokels from the hinterlands. What had they thought they were doing, destroying the alien threat, the invading horde? And they were so young—judging human years wasn't his best skill, but he would have placed them all at less than twenty. Even the leader wasn't much older. Gaurav felt tired, suddenly. He'd bet these boys had never met a non-human in their lives. Across the galaxy, how many were there, like these children? What easy prey they must be.

Gaurav had hoped, in his deepest heart, that this war would be over quickly. But now he was sure it would not. In the morning, he would spend a month's worth of credits, call his creche-parents. Warn them to bring all the family home, dig deep in the lowest dens. If they could, now would be a good time for the Long Sleep. If they could hibernate away the next few years, perhaps they would miss the worst of it. His family had never been fighters, not unless the eggs were threatened. Now, all the eggs, everywhere, were at risk.

"He's waking," Narita said sharply. She kept her fingers in his pulse for a few more seconds, and then stood up and took a step back.

The man's head jerked up, spraying spittle. He struggled for a moment, panicked, against his bonds. And then the reality of the situation seeped in—the crowd surrounding, his men knocked out. When his eyes leapt to the computer screens and saw them black and silent, he let out a low, angry groan, and as if involuntarily, struggled in his bonds once more. But Amara had tied those knots, and tied them tightly. Gaurav could see the rough cords cutting into the man's flesh, abrading the skin, remorseless. Finally, he stopped struggling, those his eyes still burned with anger and defiance.

Amara spoke, as if by common consensus. "What is your name?"

He hesitated, and then shrugged, as if it didn't matter. "Dhir."

"Just a first name?"

"You don't need the rest."

"Why?" That was the important question, after all. The one they were all waiting to hear the answer to.

Dhir swore. "Dammit. This was supposed to be the foolproof back-up plan. If we'd just stuck with the bombs instead…" His wrists were bound together in front of him; his hands clenched and unclenched, convulsively.

"What bombs?" Amara asked.

The man shook his head, refusing to elaborate, but Gaurav didn't need him to. He could see the bomb, the fragments of it, scattered across the university square. Along with a shattered flyer, and bits of flesh and blood and bone.

"Hey, mister policeman—ease down." That was Kimsriyalani, her hand on his shoulder, squeezing tightly. He barely heard her over the rage washing his eyes red, the beat of his blood drumming in his ears. This was the one. He was sure of it. This was the one who had set the bomb that killed his partner. It would be easy, so easy, to tear his head off. Gaurav's claws were already out, and he fought to pull them back in.

Her hand was warm against his shoulder, his back. He could smell her, hot and dusty, sharp, like bottled lightning. It was good she'd used his title, not his name. He'd needed the reminder. He was a policeman, a cop. Even if Gaurav were just a security guard for the university, he had made promises, to protect the people, to follow the law. He had broken those promises enough for one night already. This man was bound, no immediate threat; if Gaurav killed him, it would be murder.

Dhir staggered to his feet, and most of the crowd took a step back in response. Amara held her ground; Gaurav stepped forward. Oh, all he needed was a reason, an excuse. But the man did nothing else, just stood there, swaying.

"Dhir," Amara said. "We've shut down your missiles; your men are bound, and we're turning all of you over to the cops. If there's anything else you'd like to confess, now's the time." She was frowning, though Gaurav didn't know why she was still pushing. They'd won, hadn't they?

That was when he saw it. The moment of decision in the man's eyes, turning them black and cold as ice. The swift slide of Dhir's hand into his pants pocket—and oh, of *course* they hadn't searched him first, of course they'd bound his hands in front instead of behind; these were civilians, they didn't know any better. It was Gaurav's fault, whatever Dhir was about to do, Gaurav's fault for not noticing, not thinking clearly. It had been such a long and terrible night. He was so tired. Even now, Gaurav couldn't think what Dhir might be doing—was it a weapon in his pants? A remote detonator? Might they still, after all this, fail completely? Whatever it was Dhir was attempting, it couldn't be allowed. For the sake of these people, the children, the eggs in their nests.

Gaurav hurled himself forward, across the small space, grabbed the man in a tackle and hurled them both across the room, tumbling across the floor, limbs flailing, taking him as far from the others as he could. There wasn't time to think, but Gaurav didn't have to. Rage had already lifted him up, lent power and speed to his muscles. As for decisions—he'd made them all earlier this night. When he'd chosen to run *toward* the first explosion, when he'd chosen to stay and fight for these people, instead of going home.

There wasn't time to think of any of that, though. There was the run, the hit, the tumble, the fall. And then, the explosion, the shouting, and silence falling.

There was no time for anything more.

Esther woke to echoing sobs, the thud of her blood in her ears, the banging of a metal pipe against the ceiling in angry, irregular rhythm. She raised her head to find a disaster—one corner of the room blown out completely, scorches marking the edges of the blast. It was easier looking at the room than at the people. The bodies on the floor, which someone had neatly pulled into a row, though they had not yet had the decency to cover them with a cloth. She would not look, would not count them. Not yet. Instead, she took inventory of herself. Limbs intact. No gaping wounds. A persistent ringing in her ears—although maybe that was real. She couldn't tell. Clothes smoky, but mostly whole. Tiny cuts on her arms and face—not that she could see her face, but she could feel the aches. Clotted already—she must have been out for a while. From shards of debris, mostly likely. She could run the engineering analysis in her head, could calculate the force of the explosion that would do such damage. A self-destruct, apparently—what could have motivated the man, that he would kill himself, rather than be captured? Did he hate so fiercely, or was there more to it than that? They would likely never know; Esther read more than was good for her, and though she'd never lived through a war herself, she had read the histories of her people; she knew a little of what they had endured. Her own life had been untouched by violence until this moment. When, a few hours ago, Suresh had turned to her, the both of them naked and slick with sweat, in their new-made marriage bed—when he told her what their pandit's wife had sent along the link, Esther had wanted to retreat. Just for a moment. But instead she had urged him to go, had insisted that she would come as well. That was what marriage was, after all—to be made one flesh, in one community. They had not quite sorted all the ramifications of that in their whirlwind affair and courtship; they had only gone so far as to decide that they would follow their own religions, educate the children in both, and let them make their own decisions when the time came. They had planned on lots of children. She could have them still, if she wanted. His genes were on file, prudently saved in case of disease or disaster. If he had lost a limb, they could indenture themselves to pay for the replacement. But Suresh had lost more than a limb. He lay across the room, in the row of the dead, and maybe they were wrong, whoever had placed him there. But the doctor was working fiercely on another patient, her partner assisting, breathing and pounding and crying. And all around the room there was frantic motion, except for that one place, that row of the dead, which was so silent and still. If Esther had known, she would have surrendered pride, and honor, and everything Suresh loved about her. She would have let the Warren burn, and not lifted a finger. Anything to keep him safe.

Part V: After the Clouds

Post nubila phoebus:
After the clouds, the sun.

Day Breaks

Amara huddled on a stone park bench, her legs pulled up tight to her chest, arms wrapped around them. She was freezing and still drenched, though at least the sun was shining now. A weak, morning sun, but she would take it. A sky unmarred by missiles arcing overhead. "I still can't believe that Dhir was a professor here. Assistant Professor Dhir Vasananathan, Computer Science." She kept turning over the pieces of the puzzle in her mind, trying to make sense of them. They still knew so little, and they might never learn all the truth. She found that thought…difficult.

Narita sat erect beside her, feet planted on the ground—she was covered with dried filth and blood, but she looked as poised as if she were at temple, listening to the pandit's lesson and absorbing it in peace. There lay perhaps a finger-width of distance between them. She said, "He taught here years ago, before marrying and moving off-planet. That's what the captain said. I guess that explains how Dhir got access."

Amara frowned. "Maybe. They must have changed his codes when he left…"

"But who knows what kind of back-door access he left running?"

Amara shook her head. "Wouldn't that mean he'd been planning this all along? That makes no sense…"

Narita shrugged. "Sweetheart, I don't know that we'll ever really know the whole story. There are big players in this game, important people, with a lot more wealth than even my family has. You and I—we're just ordinary people. Pawns for them to move around the gameboard."

"Pawns who rebelled," Amara said sharply.

Narita smiled. "It's true. You don't make a very good pawn. I always envisioned you more as a queen. Like your mother, ruling your own little kingdom."

Amara winced a bit at the thought. She had led all these people tonight. Led some of them to their deaths. Would her mother have done that? "Amma rules through love, you know. That's why all those people answered the call tonight—despite her sharp tongue, they love her." And they loved Amara too, some of them, at least. Gods, she was so cold. "It doesn't seem right, that it's stopped raining." It should be raining. The sky should be grieving with them.

Narita shrugged. "They've repaired the weather system. The first missile—"

"—the only missile." She could be proud of that, at least. Could cling to it. She was so tired. But she couldn't imagine going home, going to sleep. Wherever home was. Amara couldn't go back to Rajiv's apartment.

Narita agreed gently, "The only missile. Apparently it knocked out part of the system."

After the police came, Narita had tuned back into the net to pick up the news and the weather report; Amara couldn't bear to reconnect yet. The world was still, for the most part, going along normally. The police had taken over on their arrival, had eventually released them, temporarily, after taking their recorded statements. Gaurav had had a fancy internal recorder transmitting throughout, it seemed; standard police procedure, and its review confirmed their accounts. Amara was grateful for that; she didn't think she could have borne it, if they hadn't believed her. Not after all of that. "No weather control—hence the storm."

Narita turned to her. "You didn't talk like that before."

Amara raised an eyebrow—even that felt like it took effort. "What, 'hence?' I guess marrying an English professor was good for something, even for me."

She frowned. "Don't do that to yourself."

Amara shrugged. It was hard to feel like it mattered what she thought of herself, said about herself. Not now. They had lost seventeen people tonight, almost all of them people she'd known her whole life, aunties and uncles and friends. Plus two of the devada-sis. And Gaurav. If it weren't for Gaurav taking the worst of the blow with his thick body, the explosion might have brought the roof down and killed them all.

Narita leaned in, put her hand on Amara's knee and shook it gently. "I'm serious. If we're going to be living together, I can't be havin' with that kind of nonsense."

"Since when do you talk like that?" Amara said, bewildered. Narita sounded like the peasants from the hinterlands, accent and all. As for the rest of what she'd said—it wasn't worth responding to. She didn't mean it.

Narita blushed, her dark skin flushing even darker. "It's some-thing my great-granny used to say. She was from Old Europe, you know. I wish you could have met her—she wasn't a Firster, but she also didn't see the point of humodding, not beyond curing the worst of the diseases. She always said that if she didn't earn it with her own sweat and tears, it didn't count for much."

"Well, we had plenty of sweat and tears tonight." Amara's head still ached from all the crying she'd done, as she tried her best to play nurse to Narita's almost-doctor. Narita hadn't shed a tear, but Amara couldn't seem to help herself. The tears just poured down her cheeks, but at least they hadn't stopped her. Wrapping band-ages, applying pressure, breathing when needed. They had saved a few, Narita thought. The medics that finally arrived seemed to agree.

Narita managed a smile. "Great-grandma would have been proud."

Amara shook her head. "I'm not. I could have been so much smarter about it all. Sweat and tears are well enough, but did your grandmother say anything about using your brain too? Gods. If I had just left them all behind!" That was the worst of it. That they hadn't been needed in the end, all those people. They could have done it with just two, in the end: Amara to pump, Rajiv to open the doors. If they'd tied everyone up properly, while they slept, they could have called the cops and handed them over. But no, she

had to wake Dhir up, just
because she *felt* like something else was wrong. And
it was, but the cops could
have handled it so much
better than they had. Amara
could feel herself starting
to shake now, and she
tightened her arms around
her legs, trying to still the
tremors. Hadn't they had
enough drama for one
night?

"Hey," Narita said. Her hand had lingered on Amara's knee,
and now she squeezed lightly. It didn't seem to help; Amara
couldn't seem to stop the shaking. After a moment, Narita slid
closer, put an arm around her, pulled her in tight. She was warm;
that was something. That was a lot.

After an endless time, the tremors finally eased. Amara stayed
there, her head resting on Narita's shoulder. It felt good, resting
there. Felt right.

Narita said softly, "You couldn't have known. Neither could I.
We had no idea what we were facing, who would be needed—we
took everyone, everything we could. Everyone who came knew
what they were risking."

"They didn't understand."

Narita shook her gently. "They chose to come. Don't take that
away from them. In the midst of all this madness, they volunteered
to do what they could to help. If anything's going to get us through
this war and out the other side, it's people like them."

Amara sighed, and felt a little of the grief and guilt and pain
leave her with that sigh. "All right. Fair enough." She knew, in her
head, that her second-guessing was pointless. She did know that.

"You were amazing," Narita said softly. "I would never have
thought we could do it; I was ready to give up. You pulled us

through." She hesitated, and then said, "I was serious about what I said before. About us. I don't know whether we have a chance of making it work. But I'd like to try."

Amara's throat tightened; Narita sounded like she meant it. It felt wrong, to be happy, after this night, with everything that was still to come. Twelve hours ago, Amara had left her marriage, walked out on her husband and into the night. She'd been through a roller coaster of emotions since then, confusion and terror, determination and grief. And now, what was this, surprising and unlooked for? It might be happiness, landing like a bird in her hands. Small and fragile and shining bright. She didn't deserve it. "I left you. I abandoned you." Amara tried to make the words as clear and blunt as she could. On this chill morning, she had nothing to offer but the truth.

"Well. I hated you for a long time." Narita shrugged, her arm shifting around Amara's shoulders. "But that was a long time ago. And somehow, despite your leaving and me hating and all—" Her voice dropped to almost a whisper, "—I just don't think our story's done. Not yet."

Narita took her hand from Amara's knee, and hesitantly, put it on her cheek, turning her head gently, so they faced each other. "Chieri was right. I love you. Don't understand it, can't explain it. But there it is." And then she bent, and kissed her. Lips tasting of smoke and sweat and salty tears—but sweetness too, under it all. Amara froze for a moment—and then she was kissing back, her mouth opening beneath Narita's, soft and yearning. Suddenly eager. Frantic. Narita's hands moved on her body, sliding across bare skin at the waist, under sodden sari blouse. Lightning flashed across the sky—the weather wasn't completely under control yet. Or maybe Amara had just imagined it. That was possible—suddenly, anything seemed possible, even that someday soon, they would be clean, and dry, and naked in a bed. With a window open to catch a warm breeze, and sunlight pouring over tangled brown limbs.

Then Amara could show Narita how sorry she was, for the wasted years. She would kiss every inch of perfect skin, learning it all over again, worshipping it with hands and mouth. It would be strange, surely, to see the marks of age on her own body, and none on Narita's. But Amara couldn't believe that it would matter, not after this night, after what they'd done together. None of the differences mattered. Even her mother would come around. And who knows—maybe, someday, there might be children. Amara hadn't wanted them with Rajiv, but now she thought that had been less about the children themselves, and more about being with the wrong person. Would it be selfish, to bring children into a world at war? Or could having children, raising them well, be another way of fighting for a better future?

A conversation for another day, and that clean bed would have to wait as well. For now, there was just the cold stone bench, the thudding of her heart, the warmth of Narita's mouth, moving over hers. Hands cupping breasts, brushing against taut, hungry nipples. Gods. All the gods must surely approve of this—this joy. Pulse racing, fingers digging into chilled flesh, pulling her close, as close as they could get, here in the naked dawn. Anyone could come along, could see them here—but despite what her mother would say, Amara simply didn't care.

Now Narita's hands moved between her breasts, unhooking the grimy sari blouse, freeing Amara's small breasts to the morning sun. Narita bent down to take a cold tip in her warm and moving mouth, and at that, Amara bit her bloodied lip, sparks shooting through her, running down her spine, a blaze igniting. She tangled her fingers in Narita's dirty, disheveled hair, urging her on.

Sorrow lingered, a cold stone in the pit of Amara's stomach, for Gaurav and the others. It would take time to wear that stone away. But Jequith, his mates, and the baby had survived. Uncle Karthik was recovering well in hospital, with Aunty Vani by his side. Her mother was safe, and the Warren survived, host to thousands of living souls. They had made it through the night, through to the brightening dawn.

The future was uncertain, but wasn't it always thus? Here, in this moment, was joy.

End

The Stars Change

The night air
thick as a brick
crackles and chokes.
Past echoes
hammer in the dark.

Old friends meet
in the house of God
seeking clarity
amidst the shouting.

Slowly we gather
sparks fly
and brightly blaze.

Phoenix rises
dragons fall.

Day breaks.

On The Mottoes

The title and section headers for this book were taking from a variety of university mottoes.

- University of Sydney. *Sidere mens eadem mutato*: The stars change but the mind remains the same.
- University of Liverpool. *Haec otia fovent studia*: These days of peace foster learning
- Visvesvaraya Technological University. *Modalu monavanagu*: Above all, be human
- New University of Lisbon. *Omnis civitas contra se divisa*: All the city divided against itself will not remain.
- Hacettepe University. *Times hominem unius libri*: I fear of a man with a single book.
- University of Zulia. *Post nubila phoebus*: After the clouds, the sun.

Acknowledgments

First and foremost, I must thank each and every one of the hundred and sixty-eight Kickstarter donors who made this book possible. Without you, literally, it would not have been written. Crowdfunding is an amazing thing.

I'd like to also thank Cecilia Tan and Circlet Press, for picking up the book just before I was about to dive into trying to print and distribute it myself, freeing me to go back to writing the next book, thank the gods. Circlet published my very first story, twenty years ago, and I'm so happy to return to them with this book. Cecilia, in particular, is the kind of editor who seems to get everything you're trying to do, even the things you didn't realize you were trying to do until she tells you you're doing them, and then you say, "Oh! Of course! That's the most important part!" Finding an editor like that—well, every writer should be so lucky.

My illustrator Jack Kotz was an utter joy to work with—I was thrilled to find such a talented artist. He was a consummate professional, and my only regret is that I couldn't afford to have him illustrate every single page of my book. Maybe someday!

My Oak Park writing group, the Mighty Acorns, looked at many drafts of many stories, and then I made them read the whole book—greater love hath no fellow workshopper, than to look at a piece again, and again, and again. I'm so glad I found you guys, and I can't wait to read all your books, so finish them already, okay? That's Allison Baxter, Julie Chyna, Dan Giloth, Diane Maciejewski, Holly McDowell, Elaine Marzal, and Angeli Primlani. Watch for those names! Special shout out to fellow writer and critiquer Lori Rader Day, whose first novel, *The Black Hour*, is forthcoming Summer 2014. It's awesome. You should read it.

Many others offered thoughts and critique along the way—I will undoubtedly miss a few, but among those who sent notes were Roshani Anandappa, Kate Bachus, Ingrid de Beus, Serge Broom, Catherine Coe, Thida Cornes, C.J. Czelling, Lori Rader Day, Jeremy Frank, Jeanne Fredriksen, Marg Frey, Alex Harman, Jed Hartman, Jonathan Marcus, David Moles, Kat Tanaka Okopnik, Dan Percival, Angeli Primlani, Benjamin Rosenbaum, Ellen Keyne Seebacher, Angela Sinclair, Jennifer Stevenson, and Stan Warren. Whew!

Finally, let me take a moment to thank my sweetie, Jed Hartman, and my partner, Kevin Whyte. Kevin and I had a daughter in 2005, and a son in 2007, and for a long time, I would have said my sexual orientation was "tired." If you had asked me, in that long dark time of the children's infancy, whether I would ever write erotica again, I think I would have laughed, if I could have summoned the energy. Thanks, guys, for being patient with me. On all fronts.

This book is dedicated to Aparna Sharma, a donor and friend who passed away before she could see the finished version. She sent me e-mail the day after the book was funded, saying that she'd been staying up watching the Kickstarter counter rise, biting her nails, ready to donate more to get me over the top. Aparna was a tremendous supporter of the arts, and a visionary who fought tirelessly to build community and forge a better future for us all. I know if she'd been there in Uma's house that day, Aparna would have been the first one to raise her voice in support of the Warren. I like to think she would have liked this book.

Kickstarter Supporters

The Stars Change was originally funded through a Kickstarter grant, a form of crowd-sourcing. These donors made it possible for me to set aside the time to write this book, and I am immeasurably grateful for their generosity and faith in me and my work. Without them, this book wouldn't exist. It continues to astonish me, what we are capable of, when we come together as a community.

Chip Ach
Sharbari Ahmed
Nilofer Ahsan
Laura Almasy
Camille A
Aparna
apathyjane
Matt Austern
Hawyee Auyong
Karen Babich
Sanchita Basu
David P. Bellamy
Christian Berntsen
Nova Bhattacharya
Bill Bodden
meriko borogove
Suzanne F. Boswell
Serge Broom
constance burris
Candra
Tom Cardarella
Cristina Chopalli

Julie Chyna
Shannon J. Clark
clwaller
L.J. Cohen
Brenda Cooper
Thida Cornes
Rose Curtin
curtis
Leah Cutter
Patrick Donlon
John R. Dougan
Cathy Doyle
Dawn Earp
Amal El-Mohtar
Emilly
Shannon Farley
John Fiala
Amy Finkbeiner
Matt Frank
Jeanne E. Fredriksen
Sugi Ganeshananthan
Bill Gawne

Rodney Gay
Alicia E. Goranson
Anne K Gray
Jackson Grey
Dorian Greyscale
Anne Groves
Steve Gold
Alicia E. Goranson
Sapna Gupta
Alex Gurevich
Janet
Jarmila
Minal Hajratwala
Michael Hannemann
Christopher Harrison
Rachel Hart
Jed Hartman
Andrew Hatchel
Liz Henry
Jeff Hildebrand
Luauanna Hill
Huzefa

Ixchel
Jeanne
Joyce
Karen
Keanon
Keyan
Martha Kight
Pat Kight
Alan Jaffray
Mithila Jegathesan
Lenore Jean Jones
Mack Knopf
Karin L. Kross
Joseph Lantis
Aaron Lav
Tracy Lee
Leo
David Lewis
Sarah Liberman
Karawynn Long
LongHairedWeirdo
Lori
Joanna Lowenstein
Zed Lopez
Daniel Lyke
Big Ed Magusson
Michael Maltenfort
Jon Marcus
Alison Marlowe
Nyani Martin
Angeline Martyn
Joy Maul
Elizabeth R. McClellan
Kam McCowan
Megiavelli

Ben Meginnis
Joanne Merriam
Jon Monteverde
moonshadow70
Jeffrey Morris
Michelle Murrain
Mark Musante
Niall
Livia Nocounterspace
Dave Orr
Anika Palm
Ben Parzybok
Dan Percival
Tim Pierce
Angeli Primlani
Ligy Pullappally
Mahmud Rahman
Shruthi Reddy
Alexander Reid
Nobilis Reed
Lakshmi Rengarajan
Sendhil Revuluri
Leonard Richardson
Carl Rigney
Mya Rorer
Sara Saab
Kirsten Saunders
Michael Schiffer
Wendy Shaffer
Sharmila
Heather Shaw
Shmuel
Rachel Silber
Angela Sinclair
Kim Singer

Amy & Josh Smift
Sorrel
Darren Stalder
Brad Steffen
Elf Sternberg
Catherine
    Stevenson
Judith Strauser
Swati
Jennifer Tani
Doreen Taylor
Threemoons
Creatrix Tiara
David Tidaback
Chrysoula
    Tzavelas
Carol Ullmann
Kirsten Unger
Sachin Waikar
Nicole Walker
Dean Wagner
Jason Ward
Philip Weiss
Alex Wells
Widney Woman
Brian Williams
Andrew Wilson
BD Wilson
Emily Winch
Cliff Winnig
Stefanie Zinke

About the Author

Mary Anne Mohanraj is the author of *Bodies in Motion*, Sri Lankan-American linked stories (HarperCollins), as well as nine other titles. *Bodies in Motion* was a finalist for the Asian-American Book Awards and has been translated into six languages. She has also written *Silence and the Word, The Best of Strange Horizons* (ed.), *Aqua Erotica* (ed.), and *The Poet's Journey* (a children's fantasy picture book), among others. Mohanraj received an Illinois Arts Council Fellowship in Prose (2006).

Mohanraj lives in Chicago, where she teaches creative writing and post-colonial literature at the University of Illinois; she also taught at the Clarion workshop in 2008. She is a graduate of Clarion West, and holds an MFA and a Ph.D. in creative writing. Mohanraj founded and served as editor-in-chief from 2000–2003 for *Strange Horizons*, a Hugo-nominated speculative fiction magazine (www.strangehorizons.com). She also founded and served as editor-in-chief from 1998-2000 for *Clean Sheets*, one of the foremost online erotica magazines (www.cleansheets.com). Mohanraj currently serves as Director of the Speculative Literature Foundation (www.speclit.org), which offers a variety of grants and resources for science fiction and fantasy writers and readers.

Mohanraj is currently working on *The Shattered Island*, a fantasy novel set in the midst of a brutal ethnic war, in a land based on ancient Sri Lanka. Mohanraj lives in Oak Park, just outside Chicago, with her partner Kevin, her two small children, and a sweet dog.

www.maryannemohanraj.com

About the Illustrator

Jack Kotz is a comic artist and illustrator who lives in Minneapolis. Holding a Bachelor's Degree of Fine Arts in Comic Illustration from the Minneapolis College of Art & Design, Jack works multiple freelance jobs while illustrating his first graphic novel, *Siamese*, with writer Lucas Munson. *The Stars Change* is his first published work.

If you enjoyed this book published by Circlet Press, Inc. you might enjoy some of our other books, as well.

One Saved to the Sea by Catt Kingsgrave
Winner of the 2012 Rainbow Award for Lesbian Paranormal Fiction! In the Orkney Islands, seals shed their skins to dance on land. Lighthouse-keeper's daughter Mairead has watched the selkie girls secretly and longs to join them. But a selkie girl has been watching her, too. What wildness will the shapeshifter draw her into? One Saved to the Sea by Catt Kingsgrave will sweep you away to a past that never was, and into a love story just this side of impossible.

Nymph by Francesca Lia Block
Francesca Lia Block (Weetzie Bat, Dangerous Angels) now gives her grown-up fans some bedtime reading of their own with this erotic, dreamlike collection. Interconnected short stories of subtle magic and the transformation and healing power of eroticism.

Extraordinary Deviations: Transgender Erotica by Raven Kaldera
The common conception of gender is turned on its head in these eight sensual stories by longtime Circlet author Raven Kaldera. From the ancient Roman Empire to the future to fantasy worlds, these stories follow people in their exciting and often kinky erotic adventures beyond the gender binary.

Scheherazade's Facade, edited by Michael M. Jones
The gender lines are blurred and transcended in twelve tales of magic, self-discovery, and adventure, penned by some of today's most intriguing authors. In these pages, you'll find heroes and villains, warriors and tricksters, drag queens and cross-dressers, tragedy and triumph. Featuring all-new work from Tanith Lee, Sarah Rees Brennan, Alma Alexander, Aliette de Bodard, and more, Scheherazade's Façade is filled with surprises and beauty, and may just challenge the way you see the world.

www.circlet.com

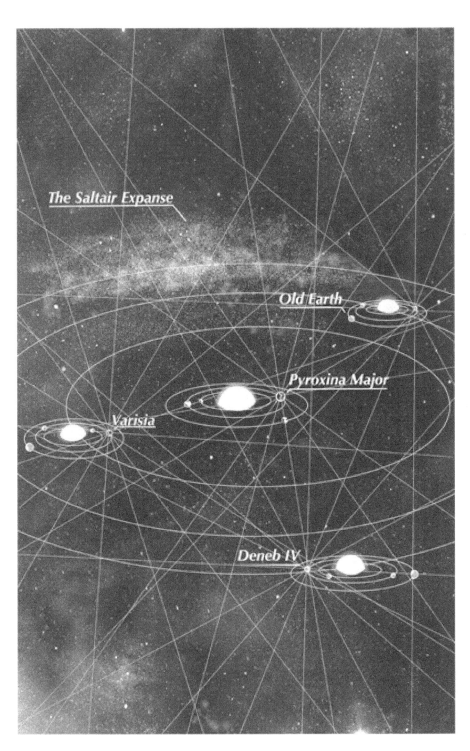

The Saltair Expanse

Old Earth

Pyroxina Major

Varisia

Deneb IV